"The problem is twofold," Spock replied.

"If we were to somehow blow the asteroid apart—and I have no ideas how to do that at this point—the resulting debris would need to fall within exactly the correct size and mass parameters for the *Enterprise*'s deflector and tractor beams to have a useful effect. If they were too large, the deflectors would not work. If the debris were too small and scattered, we would not be able to deflect it. Any attempt to destroy the asteroid must be an attempt to destroy it in an exacting manner; in the way a jeweler might break a large diamond into smaller ones. As I stated, I can think of no way to achieve this with our current technology."

"And you cannot leave it intact, yet deflected from its current path?" asked Chancellor Faber. "Use the *Enterprise* as a pushing or pulling engine?"

"The problems are essentially the same," Spock replied. "The energy required to sufficiently alter the directional vector of an asteroid traveling at one hundred and three thousand kilometers per hour this close to your planet is quite simply far more than the *Enterprise* can generate."

Merling, who had been listening to Spock's lecture on asteroid dynamics with a mixture of horror and seeming satisfaction, appeared unable to take any more. "Don't you see we have to get out of here!" he shouted to the other Vesbians. "If an alien creature such as this understands the danger, is it not clear we have no choice?"

"We do not have the choice to leave," said Hannah Faber. "The Council has had this discussion, and all understand that evacuation is not an option."

STAR TREK®

THE ORIGINAL SERIES

DEVIL'S BARGAIN

Tony Daniel

Based upon *Star Trek*
created by Gene Roddenberry

POCKET BOOKS
New York • London • Toronto • Sydney
New Delhi • Janus VI

Pocket Books
A Division of Simon & Schuster, Inc.
1230 Avenue of the Americas
New York, NY 10020

This book is a work of fiction. Names, characters, places, and incidents either are products of the author's imagination or are used fictitiously. Any resemblance to actual events or locales or persons, living or dead, is entirely coincidental.

First Pocket Books paperback edition March 2013

POCKET and colophon are registered trademarks of Simon & Schuster, Inc.

For information about special discounts for bulk purchases, please contact Simon & Schuster Special Sales at 1-866-506-1949 or business@simonandschuster.com.

The Simon & Schuster Speakers Bureau can bring authors to your live event. For more information or to book an event, contact the Simon & Schuster Speakers Bureau at 1-866-248-3049 or visit our website at www.simonspeakers.com.

Manufactured in the United States of America

10 9 8 7 6 5 4 3 2 1

ISBN 978-1-4767-0047-2
ISBN 978-1-4767-0049-6 (ebook)

For Greg Cox

DEVIL'S BARGAIN

One

Captain's log, Stardate 6397.3. We have established orbit around the frontier colony Vesbius, a settlement just outside Federation jurisdiction in the Omega sector. On the planet below is a colony of nearly 20,000 people, including many families. The conjugated orbits of the planet's moons have unexpectedly perturbed an asteroid and the huge rock is now on a path to strike the planet—and destroy the colony. Although the colony is outside the Federation, the colonists are human and have strong trade and cultural ties to the Federation. Our mission is to offer assistance and support in the evacuation of Vesbius.

The ship's intercom whistled and a look of resignation passed over the face of Captain James T. Kirk. He was on a treadmill in the *Enterprise* workout facility and was near the end of a simulated twelve-mile run to the top of Pikes Peak in Colorado. The treadmill was tilted to its steepest incline, and Kirk was sweating up a storm. He'd done this run before, but now he was working on a personal best.

It would have to wait. Kirk mashed the stop button and hopped off the treadmill as it was slowing down. He picked up a towel from a nearby rack and mopped his brow while pressing the button on the workout room intercom that connected him to the bridge.

"Kirk here," he said.

"*We are preparing to enter orbit around the planet Vesbius, Captain,*" said Commander Spock, who had the conn on the bridge while Kirk was away.

"Correct me if I'm mistaken," Kirk replied, "but I thought we weren't due to arrive for another twenty minutes."

"*It seems that what Mister Scott described as his 'wee bit of tinkering and tweaking' on the antimatter recombination unit of the warp drive has had a beneficial effect,*" Spock responded acerbically.

"All right," said Kirk. "I'll be right there."

The captain continued to dry himself with the microbial refresher towel. He reflected that while this was not quite as good as a full bath, it would have to do for now. He pulled on his tawny gold command shirt and made his way to the turbolift.

As soon as Kirk arrived at the bridge, Mister Spock arose from the command chair and took a position at his science station. Chekov and Sulu manned the navigator and helmsman posts, respectively, and Uhura was at the communications station.

It was a source of great pride for Kirk to be

among his crew. Three and a half years together had formed them into a well-oiled unit. But it was their individual strengths that most pleased Kirk, and humbled him. True, he'd picked his crew carefully, but he'd also been extraordinarily lucky to have such officers from which to choose. Now that the *Enterprise*'s five-year mission was well past the halfway mark, Kirk could not help but feel a bit of nostalgia for the times he'd shared with these people.

Yet, as always, he had to stop himself from indulging in *too* much warmth and fuzziness. The mission wasn't over, not by a long shot, and today he and the *Enterprise* crew had a very important job to do.

"Lieutenant Uhura, open a channel to the chancellor of the Vesbius colony, please. What was his name? Vader?"

"Faber, sir," Uhura replied. "He's standing by."

"On-screen," said Kirk.

Uhura pressed a button. The planet, which had previously occupied the main viewscreen, was replaced by a stocky, older man. He looked to be of European stock and possessed a shock of gray in the middle of his combed-back hair. He did not have a happy expression on his face.

"Mister Chancellor, I'm Captain James T. Kirk of the *U.S.S. Enterprise*. My ship and my crew are in orbit around your planet and are ready and able to assist you in any way."

"*Assist us?*" said the chancellor. "*I'm not sure how you could do that. Furthermore, I have to object to the Federation sending a scientific mission our way during such a time as this. Normally we welcome Federation contact, of course. Maybe if you come back in a few months, we'll be better able to deal with you.*"

"*Deal?*" Kirk replied. "Mister Chancellor, are you aware that there is a very large asteroid on a collision course with your planet?"

"*We are* quite *aware of that fact, Captain,*" the chancellor said. "*Which is why I am surprised that the Federation chose to send someone to look in on us at a time like this.*"

While the chancellor was speaking, another man came into the viewscreen field. He was shorter than Faber and was dressed in what looked like the uniform of a planetary militia. His features were a blend of Asian and European. This man leaned down and whispered something into the chancellor's ear, and Faber nodded. The other man exited the way he had come.

Kirk craned forward in his chair.

Interesting, the captain thought. Was some sort of intrigue going on below on the planet surface? Had the chancellor's power been somehow usurped? His response to the *Enterprise* offer of help would be curious behavior at any time, and it was especially so now.

"We are not here to look in on you, Mister Chancellor," said Kirk emphatically. "We are here to get you and your people off this planet."

The chancellor did his best to look puzzled, but to Kirk it had the distinct appearance of a put-on expression. *"I'm afraid there's been a mix-up,"* he replied. *"We requested no such assistance."*

"On the contrary, sir, three months ago a direct request for assistance was delivered to Starbase Twelve via a drone messenger capsule," put in Spock from his science station. Kirk knew that the feed to the chancellor would automatically pull back to include the Vulcan in the visual.

"That drone was not authorized by the Planetary Council, however. It was sent by a group of our merchants who overreacted to the crisis before the situation was adequately understood. And be that as it may," said the chancellor in an officious tone, *"we no longer require any aid, and your presence is a distraction, I'm afraid."*

Kirk touched his fingers to his chin and leaned back in his chair. After considering a moment, he spoke again. "Mister Chancellor, we've come a long way. I understand that Vesbius is outside Federation territory, but we are concerned for your safety nonetheless. I *do* have my orders. I'd like to beam down and discuss the situation with you in person."

"Captain, I really must insist—"

Kirk cut the man off. "Chancellor, Vesbius has

a reputation for its hospitality, among other things. I hope that these reports have not been mistaken."

The chancellor sighed. *"Very well, Captain Kirk,"* he said. *"I will provide coordinates for you to beam down."* The previous hard expression on Faber's face softened, and he attempted a smile. *"We really do cherish our reputation for a generous welcome here on Vesbius, Captain. We will do our best to see that it is upheld when you arrive, despite our trying circumstances. Please understand that while we are not a Federation colony, we have strong cultural and, of course, genetic ties to the Federation and to humanity. I look forward to meeting you. Faber out."*

The viewscreen went blank momentarily and then was replaced by the view of the planet below. Kirk shook his head. "What was that about?" he said.

"Curious," said Mister Spock. "While he refused our assistance, he did take pains to emphasize the colony's relationship to the Federation."

"They have strong trade ties, do they not?" said Kirk. "They are master biologists. Vesbian pharmaceuticals have been an enormous boon to the Federation. The lives that have been saved by that Rigelian fever vaccine alone must number in the billions. Plus, everyone in the Omega sector has heard of Vesbian ale."

"I am not familiar with the substance," replied Mister Spock.

"Spock, where's your scientific curiosity?" Kirk said. "It's some of the best beer in the galaxy, in my opinion."

Sulu turned partway away from his home station and addressed them. "If I may, Mister Spock, one taste of Vesbian ale and even a Vulcan might become a beer drinker." He added, "It's *that* good."

Mister Spock arched an eyebrow. "Indeed?" he replied.

"You may get your chance, Spock," said Kirk. "I'm taking you and McCoy down to Vesbius in the landing party." He turned to Lieutenant Uhura. "Lieutenant, ask the doctor to join us in the transporter room."

"Doctor McCoy to the transporter room," said Uhura into her station intercom.

Spock cocked his head. "Doctor McCoy is famously averse to having his atoms spread across the universe. May I inquire as to the purpose of including him in the landing party?"

"You may," Kirk replied with a sly smile. "It's because of something Faber said just now—that statement about strong cultural and *genetic* ties to humanity. We may need the doctor."

"Sir," Spock replied.

"Besides," said Kirk, "I had an image of the three of us raising tankards of ale and getting pleasantly sloshed together in a Vesbian beer garden."

"Unlikely, Captain," said Spock. "Alcohol does

not have the same effect on Vulcans as it does upon humans, where it loosens the inhibitions and serves as a social lubricant. For Vulcans, it merely quiets the mind and heightens the analytic side of our nature."

"Great," Chekov muttered to himself. "Having a drink makes him even more of a logical stick in the mud than he already is."

Kirk noticed that Spock, who had obviously heard the comment with his keen ears, betrayed no sign of irritation. In fact, if Kirk had not known better, he might have believed that he saw the slightest trace of amusement cross Spock's calm and composed expression.

A bleat from the bridge intercom interrupted Kirk's reflection.

"*McCoy here,*" said the voice over the speaker. "*I'm standing by in the transporter room. Since you are bound and determined to throw my molecules across space, why don't you get down here, and let's get on with it.*"

Kirk stood up and motioned to Spock. "Shall we join the doctor? Lieutenant Uhura, call Scotty to the bridge. Until he arrives, Mister Sulu, you have the conn."

"Aye, Captain," Sulu replied.

"About time you got here," said Doctor Leonard McCoy when Kirk and Spock entered the transporter room. "Now maybe you can explain to me what's going on."

"The Vesbians are refusing our aid to evacuate the planet," said Spock. "In fact, there are no indications that an evacuation has begun."

"What?" replied a surprised McCoy. "Don't they realize what's about to happen?"

"Oh, they realize it, Doctor," said Kirk. "But I think there's something fishy going on down there, and I want you along to help us find out what it is."

The three men stepped onto the transporter platform. McCoy nodded. "I would like to know what's so damn important to make twenty thousand people play chicken with an asteroid."

"As far as we know, domesticated fowl have nothing to do with the situation, Doctor."

McCoy eyed Spock to see whether or not the Vulcan was having him on. As usual, it was impossible to tell. "I'll say they don't," McCoy replied.

"Gentlemen, let's find out." Kirk nodded to the transporter technician. "Energize."

With a shimmer of dissolving atomic structure the landing party disappeared from the platform.

The landing party materialized on a wide stone veranda atop a hill that overlooked a broad plain. Rolling fields of grain stretched as far as the eye could see below them in the valley. Interspersed among the fields were a variety of farmhouses and storage structures. The farmhouses looked to be two-story buildings and resembled Swiss or Austrian chalets, with their wood and wattle construction. Winding brooks and larger streams cut through the landscape and reflected the pure blue of the Vesbian sky. Cobblestone lanes and a few wide roads connected the farmhouses.

In the far distance were craggy, snowcapped mountains. The temperature on the veranda where they stood was comfortable, if a bit chilly, and fresh in comparison to the controlled atmosphere of the *Enterprise*. All in all, reflected Kirk, Vesbius looked like an incredibly pleasant place to live—at least at this latitude in the northern hemisphere. Behind them was what seemed to be a complex of office buildings. The architecture was modern Federation, but it clearly had Bavarian and Swiss influence from Earth.

"Well," said McCoy, taking a look around, "a person could get used to living in a paradise like this. It's a shame it can't last."

"Yes," said Kirk. "It is a great shame."

"Captain Kirk?"

The captain looked around. A group was emerging from one of the office buildings, which Kirk supposed were the colony's government center. One of the group he recognized as Chancellor Faber. Another, a shorter man than Faber, was the person who had whispered into Faber's ear earlier. There were two very tall, very brawny fellows accompanying them. One might take them for a security detail, but Kirk didn't want to jump to conclusions at this point.

And standing next to Faber was a strikingly pretty woman. She was young—Kirk guessed she was in her late twenties or early thirties—and statuesque. As she drew closer, Kirk noticed that she had light blue eyes that matched the blue of the Vesbian sky. He'd never seen eyes quite that color before. Kirk found it compelling, and—

Almost uncanny, he thought.

"Mister Chancellor," he said, turning to face the welcoming committee. "My ship astronomers estimate that the asteroid that is on its way toward your planet is due to arrive in under thirty days. Since it is headed on an almost direct collision vector with Vesbius, perhaps you have been unable to accurately gauge its velocity. This is the only reason I can think of to explain why we have detected no signs of a planetary evacuation."

Chancellor Faber stood before the landing party with his hands clasped at his waist. He was worrying them together, as if under tension, Kirk noticed. But his voice did not betray any stress. "The reason you have detected no signs of evacuation, Captain, is because there are none," Faber stated. "We're not leaving Vesbius. We have decided, instead, to dig in."

"Unwise," said Mister Spock. "The vast energies

that the strike will unleash are immense. But these will pale beside the after effects—which will almost certainly be most deleterious to life. Consider what happened to the dinosaurs of Earth."

"Yes, I know," replied Chancellor Faber. "But this is *not* Earth, and we are no longer Earth men." He nodded toward the office complex. "Gentlemen, please come in and refresh yourselves. We have prepared a table for you, and, though I am very busy at the moment, it would be our pleasure to join you for a while." Faber smiled at the young woman standing near him, and this time Kirk detected only pleasure in his expression. "I would like to introduce you to my daughter, Hannah, as well, who will be joining us. She is the executive branch chief advisor for intra-colony affairs."

"The pleasure is ours," said Kirk, and he meant it.

They sat down at a large table that was made from the local variant of oak and were served by a staff of cooks and waiters.

"Don't any of these people know what's about to fall on them?" said McCoy sotto voce to Kirk and Spock.

"Doctor, I believe they know but either they don't care or they think that they have a solution to the problem," Kirk replied. "Let's hear them out. We're not going to be able to force them to do anything they don't want to do. We're out of our jurisdiction, for one thing."

The meal arrived, carried by servants who seemed carefree and well fed enough, and included several varieties of meat from the local herbivores. Along with an excellent selection of carrots, potatoes, and greens, there were a couple of vegetables Kirk could not identify but found delicious.

Spock was clearly enjoying the meal. "The Vesbians are obviously masters of horticulture," he said between mouthfuls. "And their cooking skills are considerably developed as well."

There was Vesbian ale served with the meal. It came in large tankards, and their host led the way by quaffing enormous swallows with every bite. The ale lived up to its reputation. It was hearty and flavorful, yet somehow light and sweet at the same time—veritable ambrosia. Kirk found himself finishing off his mug without even noticing it. As quickly as his drink was done, it was whisked away and another was set down in front of him.

Finally, the meal was through and all sat back. Thick black coffee was set before everyone, along with small shot glasses of even more alcohol—this in the form of a creamed scotch meant for pouring in the coffee. Kirk was sorry that Mister Scott was not here to enjoy the drink with them. The captain tipped his drink into the coffee and imitated his hosts by mixing the two liquids together with a see-saw motion of the wrist. Kirk took a sip.

Delicious.

"Wow," remarked McCoy beside him. "I don't believe I've eaten this well in years. Must be something in the soil around here. Seems like they grow perfect vegetables, make perfect beer, and"—he nodded toward Hannah Faber—"produce perfectly beautiful women. Or haven't you noticed?"

"I noticed, Doctor," Kirk replied, glancing in Hannah's direction. She caught his gaze and returned it with her clear blue eyes. Her full lips turned into the slightest upturn of a smile. "Believe me, I have."

Chancellor Faber pushed his chair back from the table and addressed all sitting there. "Now that we are refreshed as is our custom," he said, "I trust that you see, Captain, that Vesbian hospitality is just as strong as it ever was. But before we begin any discussions, I wish to show you around the colony, and particularly to show you the preparations we have made in the past few months. They are expansive, and I believe they will help allay your concern for our well-being."

Faber ushered the group outside, where there were two antigravity sleds waiting. He motioned Kirk and the landing party to climb aboard. Faber's aide, Major Merling, who had been glancing warily at Spock since the landing party's arrival, drew back and frowned. "Do I have to ride with *that*?"

"What?" Kirk asked, genuinely puzzled.

"I believe Major Merling is referring to the fact that I am a Vulcan," said Spock.

"Now, Merling," Faber intoned, "I told you to keep your retrograde prejudices to yourself."

The chancellor turned to Kirk and shrugged. "He doesn't approve of aliens. A portion of our population shares his opinion, I'm afraid. It is an unfortunate division in our otherwise peaceful society. My daughter and I are most certainly *not* among that faction, however." He turned to his other aides. "Hox and Ferlein, you ride together with Merling," he said. "Hannah and I will accompany these Federation officers."

Each party boarded its respective sled and stood on the device's surface. They held to a guardrail around the sled body as the sleds rose into the air. The transport devices were enclosed with some sort of force field, for though the passengers rose and flew away at great speed, there was no sensation of rushing air streaming past their faces. The ride was very smooth as well. It seemed to Kirk that Vesbius was far from being a galactic backwater. Even though Vesbius was a colony planet, being here was much like being back in the heart of the Federation.

After they had been aloft for a few minutes, Kirk turned to Hannah Faber and commented, "This is quite a planet you have here. One of the most beautiful I've ever seen, and I've seen many."

"Thank you, Captain, I agree," Hannah replied. Her voice was as mellifluous as her appearance was beautiful. "I was born here, and I feel that I am one of the luckiest creatures in the galaxy. I wish that you could have come at a less trying time. You seem to appreciate the finer things, and there is so much I could show you."

"So you are native Vesbian?" Kirk asked. "And you have never left the planet?"

"Oh, I have been to Starbase Twelve and to a few other nearby Omega sector systems on short trade expeditions. But those only lasted for a standard week or so." She looked over the rail of the anti-gravity sled and motioned outward. "For you see, Captain, I heard the call of my native world, I *felt* it. For a Vesbian, there is no place like home." She turned back to Kirk. "Can you understand how I feel, Captain Kirk?"

"I don't *quite* understand," replied Kirk. "But I'm beginning to."

The antigravity sleds arrived at their destination after twenty minutes or so of flying and came to dock near a rocky outcrop in one of the snow-capped mountains.

"Welcome to the Hesse Mountains," Hannah said. "I was born near here in a little chalet. My dear mother is buried in a cemetery at the foot of this hill."

"I'm very sorry to hear that," said Kirk.

"Since Miriam died, Hannah has been more than a daughter to me. She has been a help-mate," the chancellor put in. "She is extremely accomplished, and a graduate of our finest institution. It is not nepotism that led me to appoint her to her current post, but her ability."

Kirk leaped down from his sled to the landing platform surface. He turned to aid Hannah in her descent but found that she had lithely sprung off the antigravity sled and landed gracefully beside him.

In the side of the rock before them was set a large door at least ten stories tall. It hung on enormous hinges and was in the open position.

"How thick would you say that door was, Spock?" Kirk asked.

"Approximately 9.2 meters," Spock replied. "A formidable barrier."

So this *was the plan,* Kirk thought. Underground shelters. The chancellor led them through the opening and into the heart of the mountain.

It was an impressive tour. The Vesbians had dug deep. The shelter was not merely in the mountain but *under* the mountain, dug into its very roots. The Vesbians had carved a vast warren using mining phasers and hard labor. Spock provided an estimate that the space could easily house up to a third of the population of the colony, which was near twenty thousand. Under the living and working quarters were the food stores. Not only were there large stockpiles of grain and other essential nutrients in dried form, there were hydroponics labs filled with growing plants, and underground hangars filled with all variety of the planet's fauna, including a herd of the local cattle. In fact, the complex resembled Noah's Ark more than it did a fallout shelter.

"Would you estimate that they have provided sufficient genetic variety to re-create the ecosystem of the planet here, Doctor?" asked Kirk of McCoy.

McCoy checked his life sciences tricorder readings and nodded. "Possible," he said. "I think they're very near to the threshold for that. But the thing is, Jim, how are they going to do that on the surface after that giant rock hits? When that door opens up again, it's going to be a different planet out there. Paradise will have vanished."

"I know," said Kirk. "We've got to get them to see this."

"Seems you've taken a personal interest in the matter," McCoy said, nodding toward Hannah Faber. "And if I'm not mistaken, the matter has taken a personal interest in you."

"You could be right, Bones," Kirk replied.

"I often am," McCoy said. "But any country doctor could've told you that."

During the tour of the fallout shelter, Kirk was disturbed to see that Major Merling's attitude toward Spock was not a singular instance on the planet. There were many glances at the Vulcan, and most of them seemed to be hostile in Kirk's estimation. The

Vulcan, for his part, either did not notice or, more likely, he found the phenomenon interesting. Kirk, on the other hand, was bothered for his friend. Hannah Faber noticed his agitation and asked him what was wrong. When Kirk told her, she nodded.

"My people are wonderful and hospitable," she said. "But some of us possess characteristics that are . . . some of us *do* harbor an endemic suspicion of outsiders and aliens. I, however, am not among those. And neither is my father. This attitude comes from living on such an isolated world, and I think being in close communion with the planet."

"What do you mean, 'close communion'?" Kirk asked.

Hannah looked troubled, as if she had said something she had not meant to. "I only mean that we Vesbians are people who are very near to nature," she replied after a moment. "For most of us, the thought of leaving this world is akin to dying. And that, Captain, is an emotion I *do* share with most of my people."

They returned to the government center and a feast that was the equal of the repast they had enjoyed upon first arriving. Kirk was impressed with the official dining room. Often such official venues were decorated in a cold and overbearing manner, but the Vesbians seemed to be expert at setting a grand spectacle.

First there was the table itself, which was not

an indeterminate laminate but crafted of a hard and durable local wood with a beautiful grain. The chairs were large, each fit for a king. And the platters set before them would have befitted a royal feast as well. The smell was delicious.

When he was about halfway through devouring a local roasted fowl with traces of rosemary and some local herb that was its perfect complement, Kirk looked up to see Hannah Faber watching him eat.

She laughed. "I take it you are pleased with the *bürste henne*, Captain? It's a specialty of my home section. A planetary native, and entirely free range, but we've selectively bred them for their meat. The plumage also makes a matchless insulation for certain purposes."

"The taste is . . . incredible," Kirk said.

"And that's a *good* thing?"

"A *very* good thing," Kirk replied, and he quickly returned to chowing down.

When Faber and his retinue pushed back their chairs and made motions to return to their duties, Kirk decided the time had come for frank talk.

"Chancellor Faber, please indulge me for a few more moments, and hear out what I have to say. We've come a long way, and we did not travel here merely to tour your beautiful world and leave. We have been sent on a mission, to keep your people from dying when the asteroid strikes this planet. Since it is obvious that you understand this danger is looming, what I would like to do is emphasize the extent of the damage the asteroid will cause when it arrives." Kirk held up his hands to forestall any objections. "Please allow me to attempt this, I beg of you. If not for your own sake, then for your people's." Kirk looked over at Hannah. "And for the sake of your children," he added.

Faber sighed but sank back into his chair. "Very well, Captain Kirk. I will listen. But I must tell you that I doubt you will say anything that I have not heard before. As a matter of fact, you may be surprised to learn it, but Major Merling made the same argument and has long championed it to me and to the Council."

"Absolutely," said Merling. "It is my opinion that this colony must leave Vesbius, immediately. I have come to believe that the only way this can be accomplished is through military coercion. I believe that, for the sake of the people, these methods should be employed at once. This democracy with which we govern ourselves must give way to a stronger government, at least in the short term."

"Treason," muttered one of the large men who had accompanied the chancellor. And then he shook his head and said something that Kirk didn't quite catch but that sounded like "exo" or "exos."

Evidently Merling heard him and understood.

"No! I believe Chancellor Faber is the man to lead us, not some revolutionary junta. If only I could convince him of this." Merling trailed off, shaking his head. This was clearly an argument he'd had with Faber before, and had lost before. But it was equally clear to Kirk that Merling was an obsessive, not to say rigid, sort of character—a type Kirk had encountered all too often before—and that the major was not about to give up on his argument.

"I didn't say anything about needing a military government. Democracy can accomplish much when you give it a chance," said Kirk. "But I can tell you the consequences of remaining—consequences that are entailed on a purely physical, scientific basis. It's not pretty." He turned to his first officer. "Spock, can you explain it to them?"

Spock leaned forward and templed his fingers together. "Ladies and gentlemen, the captain is correct. I estimate the chance of extinction at 98.253 percent in the two planetary years after the asteroid strikes." Spock shook his head, as if considering any possible alternative and regretfully rejecting it. "Mister Chancellor, your shelters are not a long-term solution. They will not work, and your people *will* die."

Two

Spock was frustrated. Although he strove to maintain what he considered a healthy detachment from the emotional consequences of problems he encountered, the situation on Vesbius called for action. The colonists were capable of rational behavior, yet they were not engaging in it.

The science officer recalled the intense efforts that he had employed in the attempt to divert the asteroid that was headed on a collision course with the planet Amerind. It had been an extremely . . . frustrating experience. At first he had attempted to use the ship's deflectors to push the enormous asteroid off its path. When this failed, he had employed the ship's full complement of phasers to try to split the asteroid. All of this he had done while his captain was absent, lost on the planet toward which the asteroid was headed. Logic dictated the course he followed, but Spock was troubled by the thought that his friend was in the path of that asteroid and, worse yet, might be hurt and in need of aid.

He knew the capabilities of the *Enterprise*, but

he had come up against their limitations on that mission. As a Vulcan he avoided making intuitive decisions, but he had put a great deal of faith in Mister Scott based on past experience. The chief engineer always seemed to come through with engineering miracles when called upon, and Spock had trusted that Scott would be able to succeed. But he had asked too much of the ship and of her engineer; the *Enterprise* had been crippled.

The asteroid that had been headed toward Amerind was larger than the one that was hurling toward Vesbius, yet the energy necessary to deflect the Vesbius asteroid from its course had increased exponentially as it approached the planet. At its current position, there was no way that the *Enterprise* could deflect it onto a harmless vector. In fact, the asteroid had been extremely close, but not on a collision course, when it was perturbed by a conjugation of the two moons of Vesbius on the far side of the planet; the combined gravitational wells that resulted pulled it into a direct path for the planet. As a scientist, Spock did not deal in absolutes without proof. However, there had never been a chance that this asteroid could be moved to another course.

Furthermore, this asteroid was a different composition from the Amerind one. Sensors indicated that it had a semicometary structure, with a rock and ice accretion around a central metallic core. This was not an asteroid that could be split like a diamond in the manner attempted with the Amerind asteroid. It would require structural faults to do this, and the object presented no such fault lines.

Spock sought a way to communicate the dire nature of this threat to the Vesbians, to get to what, his experience told him, was the heart of the matter.

On a platter before Spock was one of the melons that the planet produced. It was similar to a Vulcan *meela,* and also shared characteristics with an Earth cantaloupe. The Vesbians, however, had applied some sort of quick-freeze method to the melon, and when served it was ice cold and quite tasty. Spock picked up the melon—this particular specimen had not been opened yet—and held it before him.

Yes, this will do, he thought.

"The asteroid that is headed in this direction is in fact a captured comet about one billion Earth years old," Spock began. "In many respects, its properties resemble those of this melon. It has a hard exterior crust and a softer, more liquid interior. Unlike this melon, however, there is an iron-nickel central core around which the ice of the comet has congealed. You might imagine that such a structure will be less devastating to the planet upon impact, but this is not the case. In fact, the concentration of water and rock is of the perfect consistency to produce multiple and widespread strikes after atmospheric entry, ensuring that the strike will produce a splatter effect."

Spock drew back his arm as if to throw the melon.

"If I were to toss this against the wall over there, you would observe the target spread of such an impact. And in fact, the pieces of the falling asteroid would be carried by elliptical trajectories around your world, and, slowed by atmospheric friction, even the side of Vesbius facing away from first impact would receive massive ancillary strikes."

Spock noticed that the Vesbians around the table had flinched, perhaps thinking he meant to actually throw the melon. He noted that if he were human, he would probably take some pleasure in this reaction. The Vesbian prejudice toward him and toward all aliens was illogical as well as a personal hindrance to carrying out his mission. Nevertheless, he must do what he could. Spock placed the melon carefully back on the platter before him and considered it.

"The Chicxulub crater, the geologic structure on Earth which is most probably the impact site of the asteroid or comet that hastened the extinction of the dinosaurs, is slightly oval, indicating an angled descent. It is approximately one hundred and seventy-seven kilometers across. This is just the middle portion of the impact site, furthermore, and the entire structure is three hundred kilometers across. Based on these figures, the asteroid itself would have been a little over ten kilometers wide and would have struck with the kinetic energy equivalent to about ninety-six teratons of TNT explosive."

Spock gazed around the table and noted the general expressions of bewilderment on the faces of the colonists. "I would offer the comparison of the largest nuclear weapon ever used by humans. This was the Soviet Union's Tsar bomb, which had a yield of fifty megatons. The largest volcanic eruption on Earth is the cataclysm that formed the La Garita Caldera in North America. The explosive yield of that event was equivalent to two hundred forty gigatons of TNT—that is, four thousand eight hundred times more powerful than the Tsar bomb. As you know, a teraton is one thousand gigatons. Therefore the destructive power of the asteroid that killed off the dinosaurs on Earth was equivalent to ninety-six million megatons, or one million nine hundred twenty thousand Tsar bombs going off simultaneously."

The science officer saw he was still not getting through to some of his listeners. "Or consider it in terms of antimatter reactions. Most schoolchildren know the story of Philos D, the moon that used to circle the fourth planet in the Beta Geminorum system. This was where initial experimentation with dilithium crystals took place. On that moon, one kiloton of antimatter was accidentally exposed to ordinary matter, and that explosion not only utterly destroyed a small-sized moon but made the planet below uninhabitable. This was equivalent to roughly half the destructive potential of the asteroid heading your way."

"But our scientists assure me that the planet will not be broken into pieces," Faber said. "In fact, while the asteroid will leave quite a scar, Vesbius is much too large to be geologically destabilized by it."

Spock raised an eyebrow. What would it take to make them understand the danger they faced?

"In under one second, the asteroid impact will have dug its way through the planetary crust, blasting up streamers of superheated steam and molten rock, including not only vaporized portions of the asteroid but the material excavated from the crater. Some of this material will be accelerating so rapidly it will achieve escape velocity and fly into space. Most of it, however, will remain suspended for a time in the atmosphere. An enormous dust cloud will form, blanketing your planet."

"Yes, global cooling," said Faber. "We are aware of the effect."

"Since Vesbius is more than two thirds covered with water, you should also be aware that, depending on where the asteroid hits, the impact will likely create a mega-tsunami that will crest at three to four kilometers in height and will move inland for hundreds of kilometers. On Earth, the asteroid that killed the dinosaurs generated a tsunami that, on the North American continent, traveled all the way inland from the coast to the middle of the continent." Spock picked up a napkin and carefully held it over his plate. "Worldwide earthquakes and volcanic eruptions will be generated that may last for centuries. Steaming new basalt plains will form, devoid of life. There will be hurricane-force winds, and wildfires will burn all exposed vegetation to a crisp. At first, the fires will create a rapid temperature rise and the greenhouse effect. But soon supercooling will result. The resulting sulfuric and carbon dioxide components in the air will eventually fall back down as acid rain. During this time temperatures will plummet. A global ice age will begin that will last for millennia." Spock dropped his napkin on the plate and put his hand over it. "You will emerge from your shelters, if you emerge, into a devastated world. A world that is as close to hell as this one currently is close to heaven."

Chancellor Faber looked pale, and his daughter, who sat beside him, seemed overcome by the summary Spock had just delivered. The Vulcan reflected that at least he had gotten through to some. But would it make a difference?

Major Merling, on the other hand, was trying to keep a smile off his face and nodding in the most self-satisfied manner. Spock thought it ironic that the man who seemed to despise his presence was also his ally at the table.

"Doomed," muttered Hannah Faber. "We're doomed."

"Not if you let us get you off this planet," said Captain Kirk.

Spock nodded in agreement. "It would seem the only logical solution," he said. "But to achieve this objective, we must begin immediately."

"No, you don't understand," said Hannah. "We're not leaving. We can't leave. But our poor world—it will die."

Chancellor Faber became agitated at his daughter's despair. He turned to Kirk. "Surely a Federation starship, with the weapons you carry, the resources you could marshal, surely you can do this. Photon torpedoes, phaser banks, tractor beams. It has to be possible."

"For a small meteor this would be true," Spock replied. "But this is no mere piece of space debris. It is a planetary body nearly twenty-four kilometers in diameter—that is, over twice the size of the asteroid that struck Earth, destroyed the dinosaurs, and caused an extinction event that nearly wiped out life entirely. The *Enterprise* will be dwarfed by it. Trying to use our weapons against such a menace would be like trying to hold back the tide."

"But how do you know unless you try!" exclaimed Hannah. "Go now! Go and destroy it!"

"If only it were that simple," said Kirk. "We have encountered technology that would be capable of deflecting this asteroid. The extinct race known as the Preservers had one such system in place within the Amerind system. But, as of yet, Federation scientists have not succeeded in duplicating this apparatus. We have been able to deflect other asteroids at times, but never one this size, at such close quarters and traveling at such velocity. Mister Spock?"

Spock considered the alternatives again briefly but shook his head. The facts added up to a certain conclusion, and to ignore the facts would be mere wishful thinking—a mental activity Vulcans found extremely wasteful.

"The momentum of the asteroid must be taken into account. The mass headed toward your planet is traveling at about one hundred and three thousand kilometers per hour, which is twenty-nine kilometers per second. Assuming we had the ability to blow it to pieces, you would still have the same mass headed for Vesbius with the same kinetic energy, only now it would be akin to a barrage rather than a torpedo. This would make little difference in the ultimate outcome. It would distribute the destroying energy over a much larger area, perhaps causing even greater damage, depending upon where the fragments hit."

"But you could deflect the smaller pieces, perhaps," said Hannah, not giving up hope.

"The problem is twofold," Spock replied. "If we were to somehow blow the asteroid apart—and I have no ideas how to do that at this point—the resulting debris would need to fall within exactly the correct size and mass parameters for the *Enterprise*'s deflector and tractor beams to have a useful effect. If they were too large, the deflectors would not work. If the debris were too small and scattered, we would not be able to deflect it. Any attempt to destroy the asteroid must be an attempt to destroy it in an exacting manner; in the way a jeweler might break a large diamond into smaller ones. As I stated, I can think of no way to achieve this with our current technology."

"And you cannot leave it intact, yet deflected from its current path?" asked Chancellor Faber. "Use the *Enterprise* as a pushing or pulling engine?"

"The problems are essentially the same," Spock replied. "The energy required to sufficiently alter the directional vector of an asteroid traveling at one hundred and three thousand kilometers per hour this close to your planet is quite simply far more than the *Enterprise* can generate."

Merling, who had been listening to Spock's lecture on asteroid dynamics with a mixture of horror and seeming satisfaction, appeared unable to take any more. "Don't you see we have to get out of here!" he shouted to the other Vesbians. "If an alien creature such as this understands the danger, is it not clear we have no choice?"

"We do not have the choice to leave," said Hannah Faber. "The Council has had this discussion, and all understand that evacuation is not an option."

"Then we must make it one!" Merling continued. "We must alter ourselves even further, make it possible to leave, save what we can, and form into a stronger, more centralized society as a result. We *know* Vesbians are better. This will be our chance to *prove* our superiority!"

Chancellor Faber stood up and turned to his aide in anger. "Now you have gone too far, Merling! You will cease to discuss these matters in front of our guests. Do you understand? This is not a matter for anyone other than ourselves to consider."

The major drew back in his chair, abashed. He held his hands up and shook his head. "Very well, Chancellor, I will do as you command, of course. But my objections stand. And I will only say that you would do well to listen to them."

"Is that some sort of threat, Merling?"

"No, of course not, Mister Chancellor." Merling let a smile play over his face for a moment and then returned to a serious expression. "I will, as always, do as the Council wishes. That is my role as a military man within our system of governance, after all."

"It is," replied Chancellor Faber. "And you will do well to remember it." Faber turned to Spock. "I hope you understand, Commander Spock, that none of us hold any animus against you. You are merely the messenger. We understand that. You put the situation in the stark terms that it demands. But it is we who must make the decision on what to do, and we have made that decision."

"Then all I can say," replied Spock, "is that your decision is an illogical one. You seem a most rational and logical people, in all other respects; it will be a shame to lose you."

Beside Spock, McCoy was fidgeting in his seat. It was unusual for the doctor to let him continue at such length without interrupting, so he was not surprised when McCoy broke in.

"Damn it, I don't often agree with Spock here. But he's right," McCoy intoned. "Let me stress the humanitarian aspects of the coming disaster you *will* face should you survive in your underground chambers. You're going to emerge into a world utterly changed. The suffering that will fall upon everyone will be immense, especially on your children. Do you have any idea what it will be like to live in such primitive conditions? The nasty diseases of old Earth and other primitive humanoid worlds will return. Cholera, rickets. Your planet developed the Rigelian fever vaccine and so many other pharmacological marvels. You must know what epidemic disease will do to a population without basic medical supplies or the ability to manufacture more! Why would you subject yourself to such suffering? You must not do it!"

"We are most moved by your pleas," Faber

replied. "We see that you are well-meaning and good people. Do not doubt that we understand this."

"Then let us help," said Kirk softly. "You keep mentioning a ruling Council. Let me speak to them. Let me try to convince them, the way we have tried to convince you. Major Merling has issues with democracy and touts the need for a centralized commander. But one of the strengths of democracy is the ability of the people to change their minds together. Allow me to attempt to change yours."

Faber sat back down and seemed to consider Kirk's request for a moment. Finally, he looked to his daughter. "What do you think, Chief Advisor? Do you think it would at least convince these good people of the futility of their request?"

Hannah slowly nodded. She smiled sadly at Kirk. "I do," she replied.

"The Planetary Council meets in two days," said Faber. "You will be allowed to address the chamber at that time. And until then, I very much hope that you will remain with us as our guests."

Kirk did not hesitate to agree, and Spock suspected this might have something to do with Hannah Faber. The captain plainly found her an attractive human—and, Spock noted, she returned the interest.

"That would be most pleasing," Kirk replied.

"But I am afraid that you will find the others as

unmoved and immovable as I am," Faber continued. "We Vesbians are a stubborn people. This was not a planet ready-made for survival when we arrived, yet we carved an existence from its rocky soil. And I believe we can and will do so again."

"If there's anybody left alive to try it," muttered McCoy next to Spock.

The Vulcan could only nod his head, and he reflected that he and the doctor were in uncharacteristic agreement.

Three

Captain's log, Stardate 4898.5. I continue with Doctor McCoy and Mister Spock on a landing party to the outlying colony, Vesbius. Although a world-shattering asteroid is on a collision course with their planet, the Vesbians have chosen to dig in rather than evacuate. What is most curious is that the Vesbians seem to be aware of the consequences of their actions, yet have decided upon an irrational course nonetheless. We are continuing to investigate and to try to persuade the Vesbians that the time has come to leave.

"A dance?" said McCoy. "Do these people have no conception of what's about to fall on their heads!"

"Clearly they do, Doctor," Spock replied.

"They'll be dancing in the ruins soon enough!" McCoy exclaimed.

Kirk found that he agreed with McCoy. Yet he also understood that continuing with local tradition was a way for the colonists to keep up their morale. He would've ordered such a dance to proceed had he been colonial governor. Still, the captain knew he must convince the Vesbians that the course they had chosen would lead to their annihilation.

The quarters they had been assigned within the government complex were luxurious by any standards. His sleeping area in Stratos, the cloud city of Ardana, had been beautiful—except for the fact that it had come with an attacking rebel from the planet below (albeit a beautiful attacker)—but these rivaled those accommodations. The bed and furniture were made of some sort of local equivalent of mahogany. They were stained a lovely color. The cushions and mattress were extremely soft and covered with intricate textiles. The walls were hung with tapestries depicting the settlement of the planet. There were no closets in this room, but there were standing wardrobes and dressers to store items. Kirk was even happy to see an exercise station in one corner with a treadmill not dissimilar from that on the *Enterprise*. Maybe he could complete that Pikes Peak run after all.

More food and beer was offered to them, but the landing party dismissed the servants. They all sat down to assess the situation around a table in the central atrium that connected to each of their bedrooms.

"I've been looking over the colony's history," Spock began. "There are some fascinating and ill-explained anomalies."

"Anomalies? What do you mean?" asked Kirk.

"The colony was originally a Federation settlement," said Spock. "There is no indication that the original settlers had any desire to separate themselves from the Federation. In fact, several were retired Starfleet officers of the era, mostly science officers—and many of them biologists. But fifteen standard years ago the Vesbians initiated proceedings to legally separate from the Federation."

"What were the reasons?" asked McCoy.

"Unclear," said Spock. "But they appear to coincide with the period when the first children were born in the settlement. The official reason for separation was put down as the refusal to uphold and maintain Article 17 of the official Federation Homestead Act."

"And what, pray tell, would that be?" asked McCoy.

"It is the article that prohibits any manipulation of the human genome, Doctor. I would think you might be familiar with it. It relates back to Earth's history, and the Eugenics Wars. It was assumed that Vesbius initiated this secession in order to conduct experiments on its barley produce. There were some attempts to splice human DNA into certain grains of the time in order to build into them tolerance to microbes that humans naturally resist. Such experiments were outlawed within the Federation but were practiced on its fringes for a number of years. These proved to be inefficient, ineffective, and unprofitable. The line of research was eventually dropped. In any case, Vesbius never reapplied for admission to the Federation. Nevertheless, it maintains extensive trading ties to the entire Omega sector, and most people do not realize it is not a Federation colony."

"Kind of like being a Canadian in North America," said Kirk.

"I'm afraid I'm unfamiliar with that comparison," Spock replied.

"Never mind," said Kirk. "The point is that Vesbian independence seems to have something to do with genetic manipulation."

"That would seem to be the case," Spock said.

"But what *kind* of genetic manipulation?" said McCoy. "Is it in the plants—or is it in *them*?"

"I believe I can answer that question, Doctor McCoy," said a voice from across the room. They turned to see Hannah Faber standing in the doorway. "May I enter?"

"Of course," said Kirk. "You will always be welcome here."

"Thank you, Captain." Hannah walked across the room. She had changed from her official jumpsuit into a gown that Kirk found extremely becoming. Its plunging neckline ended in the lace of a bodice and its blue-and-white colors accented Hannah's eyes and features. She stood before them at the table and gave them an apologetic smile.

"There is something we failed to tell you today, something that I think you need to know about us," she said. "You see, when I told you that in many ways we are connected to Vesbius, I was not being allegorical or sentimental. May I sit?"

McCoy stood and motioned for her to take his chair. "Please," he said. Hannah nodded graciously and sat down.

"When the first colonists arrived on Vesbius," she said, "the planet was as potentially fertile and as beautiful, in a stark way, as you see it today. But they soon discovered that all was not as it seemed. An extended exposure to the Vesbian biological environment had an extremely deleterious effect on humans. The colonists began to experience allergies, at first only mild ones. But they got worse and worse. Then the children, the first generation, began to die. It seemed that the planet was rejecting us. But this was our home, and we wanted to stay. Those of us who were born here never knew Earth, and we did not wish to migrate to some place new that also was not our home. So we adapted."

Hannah reached for a glass from the group of drinking vessels that sat on the table. She poured herself water from a nearby pitcher and took a sip.

"You modified your DNA, did you not?" said Spock.

Hannah nodded to Kirk's first officer. "We modified the DNA of all plant and animal life you see, including ourselves. With selective terraforming and a careful study of the local ecology, we discovered how to blend Earth and Vesbian biology into the most advantageous mix. Hence, the Vesbian barley strains that can grow nowhere else and produce some of the finest ale in the galaxy, as I think you will attest."

"It is," said Kirk. "Many things on Vesbius are among the finest."

"In the process, the Vesbian settlers became both more and less than human. We didn't just talk the talk, but walked the walk; we became one with the planet. There is native Vesbian DNA in my genetic makeup. I am part of the planet's biosphere, and the planet is part of me. As a native-born child of Vesbius, I have none of the allergies and immune system deficiencies that the original settlers had, and have to this day. Allergies that must be continually suppressed by a drug regimen. While they, too, received genetic modification, the originals will never be truly native the way a Vesbian child is."

Kirk noticed that McCoy had begun to shake with what seemed to be anger and consternation as Hannah went on with her explanation. The doctor could finally take no more and burst out with a pronouncement: "There's a *reason* genetic engineering of humans was prohibited within the Federation. The Eugenics Wars are an infamous part of human history. Millions were killed with the rise of Khan

Noonien Singh and his compatriots, the Augments. Their most powerful augmentations turned out to be overweening pride, arrogance, and aggression. That horror resonates across the years."

"We've had the distinct displeasure to have met Khan in the flesh, as a matter of fact," said Kirk. "It was an unsettling experience. He attempted to kill me without a second thought in order to get what he wanted."

"And what was it he wanted?" asked Hannah.

"My ship," said Kirk, "to begin with."

"Then Khan chose the wrong captain to dally with," Hannah replied. "I can assure you that I and most others on Vesbius desire nothing other than to *remain* on Vesbius and live out our lives here. We do not have visions of conquest, but visions of living in community and happiness."

"How do you really know?" asked McCoy, still not giving up his pique. "You aren't human anymore. What if there's something new in your genes that compels you to destroy us or destroy the worlds where we come from? You said there were terrible allergies before. What if Vesbians become allergic to *humans,* and decide to rid the galaxy of us?"

Hannah Faber shook her head. She spread her hands before her in a gesture of supplication to the doctor. "All I can tell you is that I find no such desire in myself or in the majority of my people. We wish to live in peace. And we wish to live here."

"But you would have a better life elsewhere, rather than on a dead Vesbius," Kirk said. "Surely you see that you can carry what it means to be Vesbian with you—to another world, a new world, that you can pioneer just as your father pioneered Vesbius."

Hannah sighed. "Would that this could be so, but it is not." She seemed to be on the verge of saying more but then held herself back. Instead, she rose and smiled. "I trust I will see you all at the dance? It is to be quite a gala affair. You will have surmised that we are grasping at anything that improves our spirits at a time like this." She turned to Kirk. "And please don't hesitate to ask the lady of your choice to be your partner in a round or two of dance," she said quietly, then blushed. She excused herself and, after turning to deliver a final radiant smile, exited the quarters.

As soon as she left, Kirk pulled his communicator from under the back of his shirt. He flipped it open and called *Enterprise*.

"*Scott here*," came the familiar voice over the communicator speaker. "*We were beginning to wonder if something was keeping you down there, Captain*."

"Nothing we can't handle," Kirk replied. "Status report, Scotty."

"*Well sir, we're being buffeted by this rocky churn that's been thrown out ahead of that approaching huge chunk of doom. That asteroid may be a month away, but the gravitational effects around this planet are already evident. It's churning up all sorts of debris from the local planet-moon system. We're taking a beating, sir."*

"Are the deflectors doing their job?"

"Aye, they are," said Scott, pride ringing in his voice. *"But I wouldn't want to keep this up for very long, Captain. These kinetic energy strikes can be much worse than a Klingon barrage over time."*

"Will she hold, Scotty?"

"Aye, Captain, she'll hold," Scotty replied. *"But I wouldn't make the same claim for that planet you're standing on. Not in a few more weeks, especially."*

"Understood," Kirk replied. "Maintain orbit while you can. If something threatening to the ship comes along, your orders are to break orbit and get out of the way. Do you hear me, Scotty?"

"I hear you, Captain," said Scott. *"Let's hope it won't come to that."*

"For both our sakes," Kirk replied. "Now we have another request: Have our dress uniforms collected and beamed down to these coordinates."

"Your dress uniforms?"

"That's right, Scotty. It seems we're going to a dance."

The dance was held at what Kirk learned was the colonial celebration hall. Word must have spread fast that visitors from off planet had arrived, because more than two thousand revelers packed the space. It was quite a large hall with room enough for a dance floor and a fully equipped archaic instrument band. As a cadet, Kirk had, of course, learned the rudimentary dancing skills that every Starfleet officer was expected to possess. But it had been some time since he danced a waltz, a jig, or—stretching back to growing up in Iowa—a square dance.

Doctor McCoy busied himself in conversation with the locals. A particularly lovely physician picked him out as her dance partner, and the two moved through a complicated arrangement, McCoy following her rather than she following McCoy. But the doctor seemed to be having a good time.

The captain wandered toward a large queue that led to where the Vesbian ale was being dispensed. He was about to get in line behind a group of strapping young men with very large backs when he felt a tap on his shoulder. He turned around to find Hannah Faber smiling at him and holding out a tankard of ale for him to take.

"Thank you," Kirk said. "I thought those fellows in front of me might drink it all before I got my chance. You certainly know how to grow them big here on Vesbius."

Hannah smiled, but then her smile turned into a look of thoughtfulness. "Yes," she said, "but it wasn't always that way."

"What do you mean?" asked Kirk.

"There was a generation of children before mine," Hannah said. "A lost generation. But let's not talk of that here." She took him by the arm and led him toward a large double door that opened to the veranda. They were on the same hill as the government complex; the veranda overlooked the entire settlement. Below, lights were twinkling in the windows of the chalets, and Vesbius's two moons hung low in the eastern and southeastern sky.

They stood near the railing around the veranda. Kirk looked up into the night sky and observed the local constellations. "You have an interesting arrangement of stars here," he said. As the captain spoke, two meteors streaked across the sky and left behind their paths a blue-green trail of glowing embers. More meteors fell. On Earth, Kirk had witnessed a particularly strong showing of the Leonid meteor storms one winter from a vantage point on the dunes of Long Island's Montauk Point—a spot not far from New York City. There, aurora-like plasma paths had hung in the air for seconds at a time. But the Vesbius night fireworks were far stronger than anything on Earth. Kirk gazed at the stars beyond, attempting to visualize what the normal night sky would be like. He pointed in a generally northern direction. "Rigelius there is your polestar, I see. And that way"—he swung his hand around and pointed farther to the south—"that way is Sol and Earth."

"Home to you?" Hannah asked.

"Yes," Kirk replied. "But I haven't been there for quite a while."

"You must miss it," Hannah said with a low whisper.

"I do. Very much," Kirk replied. He turned to face her.

"Imagine that feeling increased one thousand-fold," Hannah said. "That's what it's like for me."

"Hannah, I'm so sorry," Kirk said. And then she was in his arms. They kissed quickly, and then Hannah pulled Kirk into an alcove nearby that hid them from most of the crowd. Falling stars lit up the sky behind them. Hannah kissed him again, and for a long time. Kirk realized that underneath the committed and industrious woman he'd come to know was someone who was feeling desperation. Should he play upon that in order to convince her people to leave? Perhaps. But he also understood that in some measure he returned these feelings. As captain of the starship, his was an isolated position. To meet a woman who was his equal, or even superior, in level of command, and yet also so completely a woman, and so obviously attracted to him, was not something he could take lightly.

"Hannah," Kirk finally whispered to her. "You must leave. You must let me take you. Please."

At this, Hannah drew back and looked him full in the eyes. "Oh, I wish it were so simple, Captain."

"Call me Jim," Kirk replied.

"I would like . . . Jim . . ." And then Hannah glanced over his shoulder at the partygoers behind him, through the doors of the veranda and into the ballroom full of colonists desperately trying to have a final moment of happiness in the life they had built, and were about to abandon on the surface. "Oh Jim, please dance with me. Will you dance with me?"

She led Kirk into the ballroom, and as the band struck up their next number, Kirk put out his hands and the two began a slow waltz. She was a wonderful dancer, and she allowed him to believe he was leading her in such a way that their movement together seemed fluid and perfectly natural. In the moment of the dance, Kirk led himself to believe that perhaps it was, that he'd perhaps found the perfect partner. And then, with the closing bars of the music, they drew apart and Hannah gave him a quick curtsy. "Thank you, Captain, for the dance. I don't believe I have enjoyed myself so much for a very long time."

Kirk returned her curtsy with a bow. "Nor I," he replied.

And then the band struck up a more sprightly number and they danced again. Afterward, they drew to the side, and Hannah allowed Kirk to pour them each a glass of punch. He discovered that the punch was laced with the local rum, which was as potent and balanced as the Vesbian ale. It seemed that these people did anything having to do with agriculture well.

The band struck up an even faster number—music that seemed disjointed and even discordant to Kirk's ear.

"What is that?"

"Ah, you are unacquainted with our local folk dance," Hannah replied with a smile. "It is a rhythm that takes some getting used to, I'm told. But once you learn the movements, it can be quite lovely to watch, I assure you, and even more entertaining to take part in."

As they watched the other dancers return to the floor, Doctor McCoy sidled up beside Kirk and nudged him in the elbow. "Captain, I believe something's gotten into your first officer."

"How do you mean, Bones?" asked Kirk.

McCoy pointed across the room toward a corner in which Kirk could now make out the blue shirt of Spock. Several of the locals were gathered around and calling out merrily to him.

"What are they doing?" asked Kirk.

"I think they are teaching Spock to dance," said McCoy. "Though I can't be certain. I'm not even sure if such a thing is possible."

But, indeed, it proved to be quite possible. As Kirk and McCoy watched with amusement, Spock attempted a few steps to the music. After receiving correction and encouragement from those surrounding him, he tried a few more. Suddenly, almost as if he achieved an understanding of the music in his very bones, Spock broke into a lively jig that exactly matched the mood and rhythm of the music. And as they watched, a bemused Spock was drawn into the dancing crowd as others began to dance alongside him.

Kirk was surprised, but not as amazed as the locals or McCoy. He surmised that Spock had been conducting his usual study from the moment he had set foot in the hall.

"Well, I have to say it appears to be precise," said McCoy. "I'll give him that."

"It usually takes outsiders many months to master the Vesbius Tawla, which is the name of that dance," said Hannah. "Most never do. I would have to say that what Commander Spock lacks in emotion, he makes up for with perfect form."

Kirk downed the rest of his punch. "Yes, Mister Spock is most impressive. Most impressive in many ways. He's more than a first officer to me. I also count him as one of my close friends."

"Then he is lucky to have a friend such as you," Hannah replied. She closed her arms around Kirk's bicep and leaned against him while they both watched Spock finish up the quick-paced dance. When the music was done, Spock ceased moving and returned to his usual reflective self, standing in the middle of the dance floor. There was a huge roar of appreciative applause, which Spock acknowledged with a nod of his head.

"I'd better go rescue him," said McCoy, "or they'll have him dancing jigs all night. I don't know if a Vulcan can keep that up for long. He might be permanently warped." McCoy went off to save Spock, leaving Kirk and Hannah once again together.

"Captain . . . Jim . . . Come take a walk with me. I have something I wish to ask you. We could go out through the garden gate, and there is a fountain with a wonderful tree next to it. It is the first tree that the colonists ever got to grow on Vesbius so many years ago."

"Lead the way," Kirk replied.

Hannah pulled him along silently, and they followed a winding path through a series of hedges and garden displays, each as beautiful as the next in the double moonlight. Finally, they came to a large courtyard, and in this place grew what appeared to be a cedar tree of great height and large proportions. Its surface was strangely gnarled—twisted into shapes and forms that seemed to Kirk to form landscapes of their own along the trunk. Beside the tree there was a bench, and Hannah led Kirk to it.

"What is it you wish to ask me?" asked Kirk after he was settled beside Hannah.

Hannah did not answer at first. She merely held his hand and gazed up into the evergreen foliage of the tree. "We call this the Beginning Tree," she said. "It was planted as a memorial to the first generation of children of this colony."

"So it is a symbol of hope for your people?" Kirk asked.

Hannah shook her head. "No, it is not. This is a place of mourning."

"Mourning? How so?" said Kirk. He looked over at her and saw that she had tears in her eyes.

"You see, Jim, the whole first generation of children on Vesbius, all of them—they all died. It was as if the planet had an immune reaction against them and they against it. I had an older sister, Sarah. I never knew her. She was one of those children who succumbed."

"Why didn't this affect the adults?" asked Kirk.

"It would have, eventually. We didn't know at first," said Hannah. "We're still not completely sure, but after studying the planet for many years now, we believe that there is a quantum interaction, an entanglement, of some sort that the planet engages in with all the life forms that inhabit it. This process initially affects the young, but it eventually pervades the biology of everything on the planet. We do not fully understand the science—no one does—but we needed to replicate this effect. Many of the original settlers were biologists. My father is a xenobiologist by training. They knew what they had to do. They also knew it was forbidden within the Federation."

"For good reason," Kirk said. "If you're talking about human genetic engineering—hadn't they ever heard of the Eugenics Wars?"

"Of course they had," Hannah said dismissively. "This was an entirely different circumstance. The aim was not to create a race of supermen like the Augments. On the contrary, the purpose was to survive."

"They could have left, found another world."

"Yes, they could have," Hannah said. "They might have left behind the graves of their children and moved on. But they did not wish to, or perhaps they could not bear to do it. That was the choice they made. The fateful choice. Without it, I wouldn't have existed."

"No, I suppose not." Kirk considered the shadows formed by moonlight through the branches of the tree above him. Lovely. Also a trifle unsettling, almost supernatural. "And I presume that's also why Vesbius left the Federation."

"Yes, Jim."

"And then they genetically modified themselves and all new children who were born."

"That's correct."

"You aren't human."

"Not fully, no."

"Better?"

"Hardly," said Hannah. "You might even say our ambition proved our doom." Hannah turned to the captain, her eyes blazing with both sadness and determination. "This is what I want to ask you," she said. "You and Spock are friends. I have heard rumors of a ritual that the Vulcans must undergo every seven years. It is much like the return of the salmon to their native creeks on old Earth. What I have heard is that a Vulcan is bonded at a young age with another Vulcan, and that no matter how far they are separated, he or she cannot resist the urge, the necessity, to return and consummate this pair bond when directed by instinct. In fact, my information tells me that if they do not do it, they will die. Is this true, Jim?"

"I know these rumors," Kirk replied carefully. "I can tell you that nothing you told me seems to me to be preposterous or inconceivable. But I cannot speak more on the matter, for I have given my word."

Hannah nodded and smiled knowingly. "It is as I suspected then," she said. "This ritual, this *pon farr*, is real."

Kirk did not reply, but he did not deny it. Hannah leaned over and kissed him on the cheek, then leaned back and gazed into his eyes. "Now I will tell you a secret, Captain Jim Kirk. I would like you to treat it with a similar delicacy."

"I will," said Kirk.

"You see, we Vesbians who were conceived and born on this planet are tied to this world with more than emotional ties. A Vesbian must not be away from the local ecology for more than a few weeks. If one of us is, he or she will develop a rapid autoimmune collapse that will bring on death within days. And it is not a pretty death, Jim. We are writhing in agony as our bodies reject our own cellular structure. We need the biosphere of this world. We are genetically engineered to need it, and this process is irreversible. We are part of Vesbius, and Vesbius is part of us."

"But surely you can take a portion of Vesbius with you, in greenhouses, in ships' stores?" Kirk said.

"It has been tried. We have also experimented with vaccines. Nothing has worked for long," Hannah replied. "It is the whole planet that we Vesbians need, the ecology itself."

"But that ecology will soon be gone."

"We hope to preserve what is necessary to start again. It doesn't matter if most of us die in our self-dug caves. What matters is that life on this planet survives."

"But how can you know it will be enough?" Kirk said. "You're taking an enormous gamble with existence itself."

"Yes, we understand this," said Hannah. "We are very good biologists and genetic engineers here on Vesbius. I myself followed in my father's footsteps and took xenobiology as my study. That is why we know that there is so much more to learn about the universe and about life itself. But if there is any of Vesbius left after this disaster, we have a chance." Hannah turned from the tree and pointed to the stars in the night sky. "Out there, we have *no* chance."

Once again she turned and kissed Kirk, and this time the kiss became more fervent, a need that Kirk felt he must answer. The captain allowed her to draw him farther along into the double-moonlit glade, where a small stream ran and the grass was soft and fragrant. They made love in this meadow. And then, when they were finished, Hannah, as if rejuvenated by contact with him and by contact with her native ground, demanded that he do it again. Kirk gladly complied.

It was very late when Kirk returned to his quarters that evening, and he fell into bed both satisfied and perplexed. He wanted to help Hannah now more than ever. Nevertheless, he fell into a peaceful sleep, and he dreamed of her breath upon his face and her skin—alien, and yet not so far from human—upon his skin.

Four

Kirk awoke the next morning to the smell of coffee. McCoy had ordered a big pot for all of them. Kirk joined McCoy and Spock at the table in the common room that adjoined their quarters.

"Have a good time last night?" asked McCoy. "I mean, *after* the dance?" He smiled wryly at Kirk.

He knows exactly what I was up to last night, Kirk thought. *I should know to never try to hide anything from Bones.*

"Yes, we missed you on our return," Spock said. "I was prepared to go and search for you, but the doctor convinced me this would not be the wisest of courses."

Kirk nodded. "Bones was right."

"I presume you were after facts that might better serve us in completing the mission?"

"Something like that, Spock," said Kirk. He stretched himself out, loosened his muscles, then sat down and poured himself a cup of coffee. "As a matter of fact, I *did* find out something. The Vesbians are not only genetically engineered, they're like salmon or . . . like other species that are bonded to their place of origin." Kirk glanced at Spock. Even though McCoy was as fully knowledgeable of *pon farr,* as was Kirk, each of them had agreed to speak of it as little as possible. It was a matter of intense privacy to Vulcans, seeing as the *pon farr* stripped Vulcans of their treasured logic and left them at the mercy of their emotions. "In any case," Kirk continued, "if they leave this planet, in less than three to four standard weeks—they will die."

"Remarkable," said Spock. "This no doubt explains why they removed themselves from the Federation."

"Correct," said Kirk. "At least that's what Hannah told me."

"I wonder what else they've done to themselves," said McCoy, almost to himself.

"What do you mean, Doctor?" asked Kirk.

McCoy stood up from his chair and began to pace around the room. Kirk knew this was McCoy's way of working out a problem—his emotional, and often highly effective, manner of thinking things through.

"What I mean is that when you open Pandora's box, who knows what will come out?" said McCoy. "Do you suppose they stopped at merely adapting themselves to the planet? Wouldn't there be a great temptation to continue onward with their experiments, supposedly to make things better? I mean,

you've seen this place, Jim. They're master geneti-
cists. Wouldn't the temptation be to take themselves
beyond their human limitations? That's what Khan
and his people did, as you well know. And what
they made themselves into was a caricature of what
it means to be human."

Kirk got up, went to McCoy, and put a hand on
his shoulder. "You've seen the Vesbians, Bones," he
said. "Do you think they bear the slightest resemblance to that madman Khan?"

McCoy met his gaze for a moment, but Kirk
could see the fire dying down in the doctor's eyes.
"No," McCoy admitted, "not most of them." He
nodded toward Spock. "But there is that ugly
prejudice half the population seems to have toward
Vulcans."

"A prejudice Spock went a long way toward dis-
sipating last night, at least among those he met at
the dance." Kirk turned to his first officer. "That was
quite a display you put on, Mister Spock."

"Thank you, Captain. It is always gratifying to
find the opportunity to make use of one's studies
and long hours spent with the briefing files."

"Indeed." Kirk let go of McCoy and returned to
the table, determined to finish the most excellent
Vesbian coffee. "Besides, Bones, while prejudice
may be an ugly emotion, you have to admit—it's
very human."

"Yes," McCoy said. "Unfortunately."

"So we're left with a dilemma, gentlemen," Kirk said. "The Vesbians must leave this planet. The caverns they've dug are a fool's hope, are they not, Spock?"

"I would put the chances for the Vesbian plan succeeding at one in 93.275," Spock answered. "The ecological damage from the asteroid strike will likely be an extinction-level event."

"Nearly a hundred to one. Earth has recovered. It recovered when the dinosaurs died out."

"The recovery took thousands, if not millions, of years."

"So . . . not impossible, but—"

"A long shot."

"A *very* long shot. But if the Vesbians evacuate— assuming we are able to convince them and then get twenty thousand people off this world inside a month, which is a very big 'if'—then they'll all die."

McCoy sat down next to Kirk and looked him in the eye. "So what do we do, Captain?"

Kirk shook his head. "I'm . . . open to suggestions," he replied. "But we have to come up with something." Kirk drained the rest of his coffee. It, as all things Vesbian were beginning to do, reminded him of *her*.

"I will give the matter some consideration, Captain," said Spock. "I—

BWAAA AAAH!

The unmistakable sound of an alarm klaxon cut through the air.

"What the devil—" said McCoy.

The ground began to tremble under their feet, as if an earthquake were hitting the complex. The walls shook, and a nearby tapestry fell, exposing a bare section of wall.

As quickly as it had come, the rumbling subsided.

"Earthquake?" said Kirk.

"Doubtful," Spock replied. He checked his tricorder readings, rechecked them for certainty, and then said, "I believe the origin of the disturbance was technologically created. The shock waves the tricorder is displaying in feedback have a familiar signature—that of high-yield explosives." Spock looked up from his tricorder display and caught both Kirk and McCoy in his cold Vulcan gaze. "That, gentlemen, was a bomb going off."

"A bomb? Purpose?" asked Kirk.

"Unknown."

"Let's go find out, then." Kirk got up grabbing his phaser and communicator, as the others did the same.

They followed Kirk out the door and into chaos.

Bureaucrats darted hither and yon, attempting to find out what had happened and what to do about it. Kirk found the chancellor in his office, monitoring vid feeds.

Kirk noticed that the electronic equipment in the office was not up to date but was at least twenty years behind the times. The Vesbians may be some of the best biologists in the sector, but they had not kept up on the technological front. Data was flooding in from all sectors. Beside the chancellor was Hannah, looking as if she'd slept the sleep of the absolutely innocent—although Kirk knew better.

The chancellor turned to Kirk. "It appears to be a terrorist attack, Captain," he said. "It seems to have been a coordinated attack across the settlement. We're just awaiting word on—"

An intercom whistled and the chancellor keyed it on. He listened carefully to what the voice on the other end said, then leaned back, shook his head, and sighed.

"Tunnels five and seven are lost," he said, to no one in particular. "That's one third of our capacity."

"How many were killed?" Kirk asked.

The chancellor looked shell-shocked. He answered without outward emotion: "Hundreds, I'm told."

"I'm sorry, sir."

"Yes," said the chancellor.

Hannah moved to stand beside him. She put a comforting hand on her father's shoulder. "It was the Exos, Father. You know it was."

Suddenly Major Merling burst into the room. "I came as soon as I heard, Mister Chancellor. This is deplorable, but as I've repeatedly warned you, the Exos will stop at nothing—" He cut himself off when he saw that the *Enterprise* landing party was on hand.

Too late to put that cat back in the bag, Kirk thought. "The Exos, what's that?" he asked.

"You may think we are simple brewers and fermenters of beverages, Captain, and in most ways we are," said Chancellor Faber. He seemed on the verge of tears and averted his eyes downward. Kirk had seen this before. Shame. "I am sorry to say that we also seem to have grown our own version of a terrorist supremacist movement."

"What are its demands?" asked Kirk.

"Immediate evacuation of the planet in response to the asteroid, absolute separation from the Federation . . . and other items having to do with our peculiar genetics here on Vesbius."

"Evacuation and separation would seem to be incompatible goals at the moment. The Federation is your best hope," Spock offered.

"Not in the mind of your typical Exos member, I'm afraid."

"He speaks the truth," put in Merling. "It's a strong movement, perhaps a tenth of the people. It's the twisted offshoot of a legitimate political faction. Exos concerns *are* represented in the Planetary Council by those who do not believe in their extreme methods. That's not good enough for the hardcore. We believed we had the threat contained, but evidently not."

"*I* never thought it was contained," said Faber. "I knew they were biding their time. But there are so many other things to consider, so much to worry about in the coming days, that frankly even now a terrorist attack is a side issue." A light blinked on the chancellor's computer and he excused himself to take the call. Hannah Faber followed Kirk and his companions out into the entrance foyer.

"I must go and assess the damage, Captain," Hannah said.

Her professionalism in the face of utter chaos impressed the captain.

"Of course," said Kirk. "We can help. I can have the ship transport you there."

Hannah turned to Kirk, a look of relief in her eyes. "We don't have transporters. This is why we rely on the sleds."

"I have a big ship with a very big power plant. My transporter is at your command."

"You would do this?"

"Of course, Hannah."

"Then let's go," she said.

"You *will* take your bodyguards, Hannah," Chancellor Faber said. He motioned to Hox and Ferlein to go and stand beside Hannah.

So that's who those two goons are, Kirk thought. Apparently the Exos insurrection was quite dangerous, if it meant supporting a security force for the governmental representatives.

"If she goes they must be beamed with her, Captain."

"That's fine," Kirk said. "But let's hurry." Kirk wasted no time calling in the coordinates and having him, Spock, and Hannah transported to the number seven tunnel entrance. Doctor McCoy stayed behind to tend to the wounded at the government complex.

They materialized in the foothills of the mountains. Tunnel seven proved to be the same underground complex they had toured. Before them was a scene of devastation. The enormous door had been blown partially off its hinges. The ceiling had collapsed within. Hanging electrical wires were sparking, adding what light there was to the smoking darkness. Rescue crews were only now arriving, and Hannah began immediately to direct them.

While Kirk watched the young woman take charge, Spock stepped up to him and spoke: "Captain, if this *was* a terrorist attack—and there is every indication that it was—then it would be logical to assume that there may be a secondary strike."

"Someone may have planted another bomb to go off once the cavalry is here."

"Precisely," said Spock.

"Check for whatever the signature of explosive devices might be and I'll notify the ship to perform a sensor sweep."

"It could be very difficult to isolate the reading." Spock worked the controls on his tricorder.

"What do you suppose set off that series of explosions? We felt one over a hundred kilometers away. If they were pre-timed, there would have to be a signal. Do you have anything from just before the explosion on the tricorder's passive records?"

Spock quickly scanned the device's memory bank. "I believe I have isolated it, Captain. There was a strong electromagnetic pulse at 694.29 gigahertz."

"They probably won't use the same frequency to set off a secondary device, but bomb makers frequently rely on the same methods."

"It stands to reason that a broad-spectrum pulse of sufficient strength would set off any remaining devices. An even stronger electromagnetic pulse would burn the activating circuit out. My tricorder is not powerful enough to achieve this aim, however."

"No," said Kirk, "but the *Enterprise* is." He flipped open his communicator. "Scotty, I have an unusual request." He then relayed the details to his chief engineer. "Can you do it?"

"*Easy as a good scotch going down,*" replied Scotty. "*I can isolate it to as narrow or wide an area as you want.*"

"Excellent. Stand by, Scotty." Kirk closed the communicator and went to find Hannah. She was about to lead the first search party into the partially collapsed structure.

"Wait," Kirk said. "We believe this could be a

setup." He explained his reasoning, and Hannah nodded.

"I have to reluctantly concur," she replied, "but that changes nothing. We have to go in there and try to pull out any survivors."

"I understand," Kirk said. "Let us try to disable any remaining bombs. We believe that we may be able to put them out of commission entirely with a strong enough pulse. The *Enterprise* will be able to lay down a directed EMP blast like nothing this planet has ever experienced before. Will you ask your people to stand clear of the shelter for a little longer?"

"Yes, Captain."

Hannah turned.

"Fire Chief Manuel," she called out to a woman Kirk assumed was one of the fire-suppression and EMT workers.

"Ma'am?"

"Halt entry into the tunnel for—" Hannah turned to Kirk.

"Give me one minute."

"Two minutes. No one is to enter until my signal."

The fire chief was obviously unsure why her boss was ordering inaction, but she quickly obeyed orders and relayed the stop command over her comm unit.

Hannah turned to Kirk. "Captain."

Kirk opened his communicator. "All right, Scotty. Now!" he said.

Within seconds, the silent and invisible pulse was delivered. Nothing changed.

"Well?" said Hannah.

"If it worked, then you're safe. If it didn't . . . I suppose we'll find out soon enough."

"Fair enough," Hannah replied. "Chief Manuel, all clear! Let's move!"

The day became a fever dream of rock dust and the acrid smell of burning insulation and ductwork. Kirk and Spock teamed with Hannah to conduct searches using Spock's tricorder to read for life signs. The *Enterprise*'s sensors could not penetrate to the depth of the tunnels, but the tricorder was good to a distance of about five hundred kilometers in any direction. It proved invaluable.

Kirk's most intense memory of the day was when he and Hannah attempted to free a young man trapped beneath a girder weighed down by a rock collapse. The boy was about eighteen years of age. He'd been in the tunnel as the setup man for the main crew, laying out the tools and material that the workers would need when they came to work after a shift change and generally getting everything tidied up in the short break between shifts. Work in the tunnel was ongoing at this point, so the fact that the bombs had gone off at a shift change indicated that the Exos were not attempting to cause casualties so much as to bring the whole complex down and prevent it from being completed.

The young man, Balan, was completely trapped under the girder, and there was no way he was going to get out without the use of heavy equipment. Spock moved in with his Vulcan strength and, with the aid of Hanna's bodyguards Hox and Ferlein's muscular help, was able to lift the girder slightly—but not enough to free the young man. The movement did reveal the sticking point, which was the beam that had shattered Balan's knee. In the brief glimpse, it appeared he was bleeding from a nicked vessel as well, and he would not survive for long if he remained pinned in the debris.

"I'm really scared," Balan said to Hannah. She knelt down beside him and caressed his head. "I was the replacement, you know. My parents had a son who didn't make it through the die off. Then they kept trying after the modifications were made, but they never could have the boy. I have four sisters. I used to really hate having all that girl energy around, but I'm going to miss it now."

Hannah smiled as best she could. "You'll see them again, don't worry. We'll get you out of here," she said.

It was Spock who suggested the only solution, and Kirk quickly agreed.

"We're going to have to take off your leg, Balan," said Kirk. "You may be able to have it regenerated. Are you ready?"

Balan bit his lip but nodded. He looked up at

Hannah. "You'll be here with me, won't you, Ms. Faber?"

"Yes, of course I will, Balan," Hannah replied.

Kirk took out his phaser and set it on a narrow beam. He placed it extremely close to the leg he was going to cut into and lined up for the incision. Spock and Hannah's bodyguards then lifted the girder just enough so that Kirk could cut farther down the leg, taking off less than he might have otherwise, and leaving more of the leg that would not need regeneration treatment. Limb regeneration could take over two years, and the more of the original there was, the sooner that could be accomplished.

Kirk fired the phaser and moved it in a clean motion downward, neatly severing the leg and cauterizing it at the same time. Hannah pulled the young man clear, and Spock was finally able to let go of the girder. Kirk noticed that he was trembling with the effort toward the end.

They evacuated Balan within an antigrav stretcher—and then it was time to return to the tunnels and start the process all over again. The search continued hour after hour. Hannah never seemed to tire, and seeing her gave Kirk hope and the energy to carry on.

It was hours before the search parties discovered the nest of one hundred large fertilizer bombs secreted within the tunnel. The grouping was wired to a transponder that had been fried by the *Enterprise* EMP. A similar group of secondary bombs was found in the other stricken shelter.

Over two hundred people had been killed in both tunnels, with scores injured. It was an enormous blow to a colony with such a small population.

The Exos terrorists played very rough.

Five

After evacuating the wounded from the tunnels, the *Enterprise* transporter room was able to beam several of them to treatment facilities on planet—a quick diversion that probably saved their lives. The *Enterprise* sickbay also served as an outpatient facility where minor injuries could be handled by the medical staff. McCoy remained on the planet. There, the Vesbian military adjunct, Major Merling, secured the government complex and located the bomb site. It had been a smaller bomb than the one that took down the shelters, and it had clearly been meant more as a warning.

The government complex bomb had been planted under the grand ballroom of the celebration auditorium, and that structure, which had held such merriment the night before, was now a pile of rubble. There had still been a few of the serving staff inside attending to the aftermath of the dance. Five of them lost their lives, with the other nine present receiving injuries, some life threatening. McCoy, first on the scene, had treated six of the injured and saved at least two lives, according to reports. The doctor remained tight-lipped about it. He had, apparently, had to reposition a man's guts within his body cavity and then quickly sterilize and close the blasted stomach wound to prevent a death by sepsis. It took hours of monitoring before McCoy was satisfied the victim was out of danger.

By evening, Kirk wearily returned to his quarters expecting to fall onto his bed and asleep. However, Spock, who had labored as tirelessly as Kirk, was alert but thoughtful. He linked his tricorder with his communicator in order to use the ship's computer. With this, he began to run computations.

Kirk watched his first officer for a while. In a nearby alcove, McCoy was noticeably snoring.

"What's going on, Spock? Have you got an idea?"

"More of a notion, Captain," Spock replied. "While we were digging through the collapsed material to rescue that mining engineer with the head wound, I recalled another moment you and I spent in such close quarters underground."

"Well, spit it out, Spock," Kirk said. He sat down beside his first officer. "What are you thinking?"

"The asteroid headed toward this planet is too large to be destroyed by conventional means, and were we to succeed in breaking it apart, that would merely create a shotgun blast to the planet rather than a rifle bullet."

"Agreed."

"But we do have the technical ability to move smaller pieces of matter with the *Enterprise*'s tractor beams and deflectors. If those pieces were cut to precise sizes, that is. Anything too small would be impossible upon which to achieve a lock. As you know, the tractors cannot lock on to space dust. As a matter of fact, this inability is a very useful quality, in most instances—"

"Spock, I understand the technical capabilities of our tractor beam."

"Captain, I was merely pointing out—"

"Spock, what are you getting at?"

"In all our travels, we have encountered a great many aliens and alien civilizations. These have been capable of many wonders. But there is one species whose rock-cutting and digging abilities are unrivaled."

Kirk felt a smile spreading across his face. "You wouldn't be talking about the Horta?"

"That is exactly what—or *whom*—I am talking about," Spock replied. "If you will recall our encounter with the creature, it was a peaceful, highly developed individual."

"The All Mother, the tender of those eggs, you mean."

"Yes, Captain. A most logical race."

"No doubt, Mister Spock," Kirk said. "But I still don't understand how—"

"During our encounter with the wounded Horta, I was able to achieve a mind meld with the creature. As you recall, this allowed us to communicate with it—her, as it turns out—and discover why she was attacking miners in the shafts of Janus VI."

"The silicon nodules they were discarding were eggs," said Kirk. "She was protecting her babies."

"And now those eggs have hatched, Captain," Spock replied. "The rocky halls of Janus VI are crawling with young Horta who are working with the miners, with both species reaping the benefits. After all, what is a hard rock to us is merely food to a Horta."

"Yes, but—"

"I have performed the calculations. Janus VI is in the Omega sector, albeit near the other end. At maximum warp, a six-day journey will get us there."

"Warp eight, you mean?"

"Yes."

"Scotty will kill me. Go on."

"Once there, we will, of course, have to negotiate with the Horta."

"Convince a sufficient number of them to return with us?"

"Correct."

"However many that may be."

"Yes, Captain."

"But Spock, you're forgetting one thing," Kirk said.

"Am I?"

"The Horta, they're still babies. Who knows how fast they mature? We didn't even know they were sentient."

Spock set down his tricorder and closed it up. "I believe I said it was a rather unformed plan, Captain."

Kirk nodded. "Yes, I believe you did. And if we get them here, you think we have time?"

"Unknown, Captain," Spock said. "The Horta are master miners, after all. We would have to ask them. However, I do believe the task will be made sufficiently easier by the composition of the asteroid they are asked to dig through. It is an accreted comet surrounded by a shell of rock and ice, the passage of which will be to the Horta a snack."

Kirk considered. "If I offer an alternate plan in the Council meeting tomorrow, perhaps I can convince them to prepare for full-scale evacuation as a fallback. Surely we can find some way to 'de-engineer' this genetic tinkering they've been doing to their genome."

"Unlikely, Jim." It was the voice of a tired McCoy. He stumbled into the room with mussed-up hair and plunked himself down at the central table.

"I thought you were asleep, Doctor."

"I thought I was too, but with you both squawking up a storm in here like Tellurian genta bats, there was no way I could keep that up. So I started listening. You do realize how unlikely this plan is, don't you?"

"I don't have a lot of options at the moment, Bones."

"Well, I hope it works, because I've had a good look at the engineering these people have done to their genome while I was treating my patients today. They've made changes that are irreversible. I think most of them are as much as five to ten percent native, sharing this planet's odd triple-helix gene structure. In comparison, humans and chimpanzees are ninety-eight percent similar. Let me tell you, there are many unknowns about that kind of genetic structure, but there is one *known*: That stuff is not very human, and neither are the structures it expresses. In fact, I don't know what most of those genes *do*. I'm going to get a great paper out of mapping them after all this is over. But the one thing you cannot achieve with any current methodology is to deconstruct those genes in every cell and then remake a human out of the remains. These people are Vesbians now, and they're going to remain Vesbians, for better or worse."

"Then it would seem that Spock's idea is our only one."

"That doesn't improve its chances," McCoy mumbled.

Kirk had to agree. But he had to admire his first

officer. When backed into a corner, he had come up with a brilliant plan that just *might* succeed. Of course, its very success depended upon Spock and his mind melding ability.

And the Horta.

What were they like? Were they as crusty and acidic in personality as they were on the outside? Would they help?

Kirk finally fell into an exhausted sleep, and his dreams were filled with Horta.

He awoke the next morning to the urgent bleating of his communicator. He struggled up in bed and reached for the device, which lay on the nightstand nearby, and flipped it open. "Scotty, I was hoping to get a couple more hours sleep after the day we had yesterday."

"*Sorry, sir,*" came Scotty's cheerful voice. He sounded as if he'd just awakened, eaten a large breakfast, and was eager to face a new day. It turned out that Scotty had spent much of the night scanning the planet surface.

"*After that second cache of bombs was discovered,*" said the chief engineer, "*I knew what to look for, Captain. They were pretty primitive devices—fertilizer bombs, if you can believe it—even though they packed quite a wallop.*" Scotty chuckled. "*But it makes sense if you're short on bomb-making material and it makes sense if you want to hide them. The entire planet is an agricultural center, after all.*"

"Scotty, I haven't had any coffee yet," said Kirk. "Could you get to the point?"

"Aye, Captain," said Scotty. *"Well, since we did have those unexploded bombs, we were able to analyze the exact chemical composition. I've been running scanner sweeps looking for those chemical signatures."*

"And you found something?"

"Captain," said Scotty, concern seeping into his voice, *"a whole lot of something. Bombs. Lots of them. And they're all planted under the Council chamber in that complex you're staying in."*

Realization dawned on Kirk. "No doubt they're set to go off this afternoon at the Council meeting."

"You'd be knowing that better than I, Captain," replied Scotty. *"We've got locks on the position of all of the planted bombs. We were able to analyze the triggering mechanism. They've learned from their mistakes. These babies are shielded from EMP. Just give the command, Captain, and I'll beam them into space and blast them with the phasers just for good measure."*

"Do it, Scotty. Get rid of them all. And continue those sensor scans."

"I'll get on with it, then," said Mister Scott. *"And sorry about the rude wake-up call."*

"Don't worry about it," Kirk said while locating a boot to pull on. "You saved a lot of lives. Kirk out."

This was going to be interesting information to take before the Council. Interesting indeed.

Montgomery Scott turned to Chekov, who was at the bridge science station, and asked him to verify the positions of the bombs.

"We have them all logged and verified," Chekov replied in his Russian accent, having trouble, as always, with the *v* sound. Scott sometimes wondered what his own Scottish brogue sounded like to Chekov. He supposed it must be as odd to Chekov as Chekov's was to him. The truth was, to Scotty it was everyone else who had an accent, not him. To Scotty's ears, his way of speaking sounded just perfect. To each his own.

"All right then, let's beam them out, as many as we can at a time." Scotty touched the key on the captain's chair and opened communication to the transporter room. "Stand by to transport bombs to deep space. Is the security and science team ready in case there's the slightest glitch when those things appear on the transporter platform?"

"Both are standing by," reported Transporter Chief Bynum. *"They won't be here longer than a millisecond, sir."*

"Aye, but it's best to be on the safe side," said Scotty. "Energize when ready."

"Energizing."

In the transporter room the bombs materialized one by one on the platform and were almost
instantaneously beamed away to the same region in
space—a distance as far from the *Enterprise* as the
transporter beam could put them. After about two
minutes of steady beaming, the job was done, and
the transporter chief reported in to the bridge.

"Bombs transported, sir."

"Very good." Scott turned to the helm. "Weapons locked on target."

"Phasers locked," said Sulu. "Standing by to fire."

"All right, let's make those things go away permanently," said Scott. "Fire phasers."

Sulu activated the phasers, and there was the familiar power whine of discharge. To Scotty, it was a
beautiful sound, the sound of energy being properly
directed, and a problem being solved.

On the viewscreen, the bombs erupted in an
expanding fireball of pure energy. If they had gone
off on the planet surface, they would not have had
nearly this much explosive potential. The phasers
were effectively transforming the bomb material
into plasma. There was no need for oxygen to ignite
them here in space, not with a starship's phasers
blasting through the matter of which they were
composed.

The chief engineer watched as the last of the
explosive streamers trailed away into space and all
was empty again against the backdrop of stars.

Scotty realized that he hadn't slept for nearly eighteen hours. He'd been working overtime to track down those bombs. He hoped that he had them all. He and Chekov had developed a search algorithm that served as a very effective net. He couldn't be a hundred percent sure, but Scotty felt he could finally rest confident that the crew of the *Enterprise* had saved a lot of lives.

"Let's call it a day," Scott said. "At least I will. Mister Sulu, you have the conn." Scotty turned to Chekov. He could see the excitement of having fulfilled his duty still lingering on the ensign's face. He could also detect the weariness of the task starting to take its toll. "Ensign Chekov, that was some good work you did. I know you're young, but it's time to take a wee little breather."

"I don't know if I could close my eyes if I tried," said Chekov.

"I know how you feel, laddy," Mister Scott replied, "I do. But that's an order. I have a feeling our services will be needed soon enough."

Six

Captain James Kirk looked over the faces of the Planetary Council assembled before him. They appeared careworn, and not like people open to a last-minute idea that would severely challenge the direction they'd taken to save themselves.

Hannah sat nearby. He'd seen her the night before, and if anything their coming together had been even more passionate than the first time. Kirk enjoyed the company of women, but she was proving to be something different. The captain realized he was falling in love. The impossibility of the situation only made the feeling stronger. He had always had an ability to live in the moment. He did not forget the past, nor stop caring about the future, but both became integrated into his subconscious mind and did not weigh upon him. In fact, he felt sorry for Spock, for the Vulcan could never know what it was like to experience a moment unconnected from reason, and yet not illogical or irrational. Such was Kirk's feeling for Hannah. When he was with her, he truly did not think about the future. If this was what love meant, Kirk was glad that he was open to it, even if it would mean heartbreak in the end.

Kirk turned his attention back to the Council, and to Chancellor Faber, who was speaking. "Now I would like to introduce our esteemed visitor from the Federation, Captain James T. Kirk, along with his first officer, Commander Spock, and the chief medical officer, Doctor Leonard McCoy, of the *Starship Enterprise*. They've come to offer their assistance to us, and they *have* been of great help. Only yesterday, with the aid of an alert *Enterprise* crew, a bomb plot was discovered and eliminated. Many lives were saved."

For some in the Council, the new bomb plot was news, and assorted gasps and other signs of surprise and alarm arose from the chamber. The Council members—there were fifteen of them—sat in a semicircle on a raised dais across from Kirk. He and the chancellor and the chancellor's staff were sitting at a long table that faced the Council dais and was slightly below it. The Council members were, in effect, looking down upon him and he up at them, although the effect was subtle. Also at the table sat Spock and Doctor McCoy on either side of Kirk.

"It is for this reason that I have approved Captain Kirk's request to speak to this chamber," said Chancellor Faber. "He has a plan he wishes us to consider, and while I remain unconvinced as to its efficacy, I believe we owe him our every attention, and we ought to hear him out. He has earned the right to be heard on Vesbius." The chancellor motioned for Kirk to begin, and the captain stood up.

"Ladies and gentlemen of the Planetary Council," Kirk began. "I wish to express to you my great admiration for your accomplishments in surviving and prospering on this world. I am also very much impressed by the preparations you have begun in order to survive the oncoming asteroid strike. When I first arrived, I did not understand why you would not have already evacuated the planet surface, perhaps relocating to a moon or even to another planet where you could start again. But now that I understand more about Vesbian physiology, it is clear to me why you made the decision you made. But I must say, you are relying upon a very distant hope. Your underground shelters are masterfully built chambers, but you saw from the bomb blasts of yesterday that they might not withstand the kind of devastation that is coming upon you. And even if they do, even if your engineering holds, you will emerge upon a destroyed world.

"And yet I understand why you cannot leave. At least, I understand why you cannot leave and remain in your present form. It may seem that people as clever as you have been in adapting to this planet may be able to come up with a solution to adapt to another. Some would say that, barring a miracle, this is the only rational course you could take. You will not survive the coming storm, but some will say that you may, possibly, find a way to adapt yet again. I know this is a delicate matter, but it is time to speak frankly if ever there was such a time. I have no doubt you also are aware of the dangers of genetic manipulation. Perhaps what has been done, can somehow be undone."

"What makes you think we have not tried to do this before?" A voice creaking with age rose up from the chamber, a woman's voice. Kirk located the source in a silver-haired matron, who was sitting to the left on the dais. Kirk noted that her time-worn expression was belied by the softness of her speech. "If I understand you correctly, Captain," the Council member said, "you say some might wish us to remove the very autoimmune defense which we engineered into our genetic structure to save ourselves here on Vesbius?"

"I speak of modification for survival," Kirk replied.

"How would you feel if someone told you that you had to remove the ability to speak from your own genome? Or how about your ability to reason? The change others might want us to make is not the same thing as taking away a human appendix. We are intimately bound with this planet, and to take away this sensation, this physiological connection, would be akin to murdering part of ourselves. It is something that we cannot do."

"I understand you've attempted something along these lines?"

"There is an experimental vaccine. There was much debate over its development, much less its use."

"But you *did* use it?"

"Yes."

"And was it effective?"

The woman frowned and shook her head sadly. "For a very short time, and then the effect diminished rapidly. This rapid decline in effectiveness was most pronounced in the native born. The vaccine proved a dead end."

"But it did work for a time?"

"Days for some, mere hours for others. But always . . . failure."

"So that avenue is closed for the time being," Kirk said.

"It is closed," said the matronly Council member.

Kirk had the fleeting notion to set McCoy and Spock loose on this vaccine to see if they could improve it. But this was a planet full of expert biologists. If *they* couldn't come up with a solution, then it was probably a dead end for even his officers in so short a time.

"So you see, Captain Kirk, we are going to need a miracle, just as Marlena intimates," said another Council member, a young man with an intensely handsome face, dark complexion, and well-muscled frame. There was a half-smile upon his face, and he appeared . . . amused. "She may be original stock, and older than the Hesse themselves, but she sometimes makes sense."

Who does he remind me of? Kirk thought. Then it came to him: *Khan Noonien Singh.*

"Thank you for the compliment, Jasper," Marlena replied. "But I'd caution you to avoid biting your pretty little tongue by wagging it too much."

The man laughed and turned to the captain. "So, do you have a miracle for us, Kirk? Is that why you've come? If not, then we're done here."

Behind the obvious sarcasm, Kirk detected a note of fear in the man's voice.

Now's the time to spring Spock's plan, Kirk thought. *As tenuous as its prospects may be.*

Kirk did his best to direct a smile of knowing contentment toward the Council. "As a matter of fact, I do have a miracle in mind. Or at least I have a long shot chance in mind. It will require the cooperation of the planetary government, which is why I'm bringing it to you tonight."

"What is your miracle then?" asked the Council member known as Marlena.

Kirk nodded respectfully in her direction. "Please hear me out. Not long ago on the voyages of my ship we were called to the mining colony on a planet known as Janus VI. It seemed that a series of miners had disappeared on the planet. They had been killed. Missing was a shipment of an important mineral that is a key element in Federation transporter technology, pergium.

"In the course of searching for the lost shipment, we discovered that the mining colony had unearthed an area of silicon nodules. These had no intrinsic value to them, so they had discarded them. But when we discovered what it was that was killing the miners, the mystery was solved. The silicon nodules were *eggs* and the killer—the monster, the devil in the dark—a mother who was protecting her children. The species is called the Horta.

"The Horta are a very strange life form, like none other we've discovered in the galaxy. It is silicon-based, rather than carbon-based. It excretes an extremely acidic body coating that enables it to move through rock as if moving through air. When you are in a Horta-created tunnel, you see the precision with which their unique physiology allows the Horta to carve the rock. For them, moving through solid material is a natural act, an act of will and almost no effort on their part, other than locomotion. They understand the structure of rock in the same way that we understand wind and air. Instinctively.

"Mister Spock"—Kirk gestured toward his first officer, who nodded his head in greeting to the Council—"is Vulcan. Vulcans are touch telepaths; they have the ability to communicate with other sentient species via a Vulcan mind meld. Mister Spock used a Vulcan mind meld on the Horta mother and was able to establish contact and understanding between our species. In fact, the Horta and the miners on Janus VI have become not merely friends but allies in the mining process. It is a situation that went from horror to hope."

"This is all very well and good," said Marlena, "but what does this have to do with saving Vesbius?"

"Mister Spock has calculated that it may be possible for a sufficient number of Horta to precisely carve the oncoming asteroid in such a manner that we would be able to shunt it out of the way with the *Enterprise*'s deflector beams. This would be an extremely delicate procedure, and I don't need to tell you that nothing like this has ever been tried before. But it is a chance. Spock believes it has a much higher chance of succeeding than your plan to retreat into the shelters. I therefore propose that I take the *Enterprise* to Janus VI. It is within the Omega sector in the Federation. There we will attempt to recruit enough Horta to eat that asteroid from the inside out. We will then use our phasers to break it into precise and manageable chunks, and use our tractor beams to move them on a path that will not strike the planet Vesbius.

"I need not tell you that this may not work. There are several obstacles standing in the way of the plan, some of them known and some of them unknown."

"Exactly how many Horta *are* there?" asked a

younger Council member who had spoken before. "And how many do you think it will take?"

Kirk looked to Spock, who rose to speak. "Both of these questions are part of the unknown that Captain Kirk spoke of. Remember, there was at first only one Horta that we encountered, one living Horta. It was only after the eggs hatched that baby Horta came out and populated the Janus VI mining system."

"How long ago was that?" asked the matronly Council member.

"Approximately two Earth years ago," answered Spock. "So the Horta, which can live thousands of years, are extremely immature at this point. Are they developed beyond the human equivalent of being a toddler? That we do not know. From my mind meld with the mother Horta, however, I understood that the Horta are a fast-developing species in youth and have an extremely long—the equivalent is not exact but let us call it this—adolescence. So it is more likely that the Horta we might recruit would be more akin to human teenagers than to infants or toddlers. And while there has not been an adequate count made of the number of Horta on Janus VI, I estimate from the number of eggs that I observed upon the visit we made that there should be several thousand of the creatures working the mines and living under the surface.

"As for how many it will take to carve out the

asteroid," Spock continued, "I have made a very rough estimate that we will need about five hundred."

"And you believe you can get these creatures to come here and help us?" asked the older lady.

"I cannot answer that," said Spock. "We will be going there, I believe the Earth expression is, on a wing and a prayer."

Spock bowed his head slightly and sat down.

Kirk rose again. He took a moment to consider the Council. "The *Enterprise* will put your case to the Horta. We will try to make them understand how great the danger is to your world." The captain shook his head and shrugged. "I'm afraid that's the best plan we have been able to come up with. In the meantime, I urge you to consider an evacuation. I understand that many of you are opposed to this. I also understand that the terrorist group, which struck this week, is attempting to push you to do exactly what I am advocating here. But for the survival of your people, you must realize that the caves are not a viable option."

Kirk sat down. Chancellor Faber reached over and picked up his gavel, then rapped it three times on a pedestal in front of him.

"We will now put this matter to a vote," he said. "As for myself, although it sounds like as much a fool's errand, as Captain Kirk claims our shelters to be, I will support this mission."

He turned to Kirk. "*Horta*. What an odd name

for a species. But I suppose they would think that *Vesbian* is just as odd, if they were able to hear it. Can they even hear?"

"They can detect atmospheric vibrations," Spock answered. "But their sense of smell is highly developed. It is one of their means of communication."

"I see," said the chancellor. He turned to the Council and spoke in a louder voice. "Council clerk, please call the roll."

It was close, but in the end Kirk had won his approval. They had voted for a miracle. Now all he had to do was deliver.

"Thank you for your faith in this effort," the captain said. "We will do all in our power to bring back—"

Chancellor Faber cut him off before he could finish. "We thank you for this possible avenue of rescue, Captain. And to show you and the Federation that we are committed to this plan, I am going to send my top advisors along with you to help in any manner possible. In fact, if the Council approves it, I will send with Captain Kirk my chief advisors—my daughter, Hannah, and Major Merling—to be our representatives to the Horta."

Hannah seemed startled, as if she hadn't expected this turn of events. "But, Father . . . Chancellor . . . there is much to do in supervising the reconstruction of the blasted tunnels."

"Work that you have already set in motion,"

Chancellor Faber answered. His expression softened. "The damage was extensive, and it is a forlorn hope that we will get them ready in time."

"But Chancellor, with redoubled effort—"

"You could very well work yourself to death, Daughter, and to what purpose? No, it is not my wish," Faber replied.

"I will stay."

Her father stood up, glaring at Hannah and shaking his head.

"I order you to go, Chief Advisor Faber," he said. "This is the last chance to save our world, and I want my best team on it." Faber turned to Major Merling, who sat nearby. "That's why I'm also sending Merling here."

"Me? But Chancellor, I—"

"That, too, is an order, Major," Faber said quietly, but with steel in his voice. "I want you both to be available to the captain should he need any expert advice on Vesbius. And I want you both there as emissaries to represent Vesbian interests."

Kirk bridled at the idea that *he* wouldn't have the colony's best interests at heart. "Mister Chancellor, I assure you—"

"Indulge me in this matter," Faber said. "While we of Vesbius share much by way of culture and family ties with the Federation, we are *not* Federation members, and for this reason we must see to our own affairs. I'm sure you understand."

"I understand your reasoning," Kirk said. "And,

of course, I would be very happy to have these representatives on my ship." Kirk shrugged. "But Chancellor, what of the autoimmune response?"

Faber held up a palm to forestall this objection. "We will send along a supply of the suppression vaccine. Its effects vary, but its potency ought to be sufficient for this journey, provided you are not delayed too greatly."

"If we are delayed by much, the entire expedition will fail."

"Just so," said Faber.

As Kirk rose to leave, he heard the chancellor add in a soft voice: "And take care of my daughter, Captain. Whatever happens to our people and planet, look after her, will you?"

Kirk felt the warmth of a father's feeling—and felt it matched by a surge of feeling on his own part.

I haven't felt this strongly about a woman since . . . Miramanee, he thought, back on Amerind. And she is long dead now. Dead with the child she bore inside her. My child. Does this mean I have finally moved on? I can just draw further away from that terrible moment in time . . .

But to love again . . .

Kirk answered, "I'll do everything in my power to protect Hannah. That's a promise."

Seven

Captain's log, Stardate 6400.1. Having convinced the Vesbian Planetary Council that Mister Spock's plan for recruiting Horta might have a chance of success, the Enterprise *is en route to Janus VI. We shall attempt to contact the Horta and bring a contingent of them back to Vesbius. It is a risky plan with many unknowns, but given the circumstances, and the Vesbians' unique relationship with their planet, it seems our only course of action.*

Warp factor eight was the highest speed of which the *Enterprise* was capable for sustained periods. But six days at warp eight was another matter entirely. It was all Scotty could do to hold the engines together as Kirk pushed them to their maximum limit and then kept them there. Everything had to fall into place very quickly for the plan to work, and there was no time for any delays. Nevertheless, Kirk felt the pain of his ship as she groaned and suffered under the immense load of acceleration through subspace. He was careful not to show his concern to the crew. And he did not think that anyone, even his closest compatriots, were aware of his semi-mystical attachment to the *Enterprise*.

Fortunately, through Scotty's engineering wizardry and a crew whose members were masters of navigation and handling the thousands of minute adjustments that traveling through subspace required, the *Enterprise* arrived at Janus VI overheated and strained, but intact. Taking things to the extreme was what a *Constitution*-class starship was meant to do, and the *Enterprise* had responded to the challenge, as Kirk had known she would.

Hannah, her two bodyguards, and Major Merling had beamed up to accompany the ship on the voyage. Uhura had offered up her quarters for Hannah and had moved across saucer to bunk with another officer for the duration of this expedition. Uhura had taken most of her personal belongings but had left a few pieces of Earth art displayed on her walls. Hannah had made an excellent first impression on Uhura by pronouncing them charming and praising the communication officer's taste as exquisite.

"What a difference from that awful Elasian woman," Uhura had said to Kirk.

Ah, Elaan, now of Troyius, thought Kirk. *Yes, Elaan and I gave Uhura's quarters quite a workout.*

As if Uhura sensed that there was something more than met the eye between Hannah and her captain, she added, "I would say this one is a keeper, Captain."

"I really have no idea what you're talking about, Lieutenant," Kirk replied, but in a light tone to let her know he didn't really mind the teasing.

Uhura smiled and went to her station.

Hox and Ferlein, Hannah's aides *cum* body-guards, were also housed on deck five, sharing a double-bunk quarters normally not in use. Major Merling proved to be the Vesbian most difficult to accommodate. Upon beaming aboard, he had in-sisted on being placed as far away as possible from Spock's quarters, which required that he be assigned a junior officer's cabin.

In the close confines of the ship, however, Mer-ling found complete separation from the Vulcan impossible. There was even a tense moment in the rec room when Merling entered to pick up some entertainment tapes and ran into Spock, who was playing three-dimensional chess with Ensign Perkins, one of Scotty's young Turk wizards in en-gineering. The look of disgust that passed over Mer-ling's face was apparent to all in the rec room, and had Merling not made his exit immediately, there may have been trouble. While many humans on the *Enterprise* found Spock to be cold and off-putting, he was still one of them, and crew loyalty ran deep on the ship.

Five days into the voyage Merling was forced to

encounter Spock in the ship officers' mess at a for-
mal dinner that Kirk gave for his visitors on the trip
out to Janus VI. Hannah and Merling were seated
at places of honor, and all the attendees wore dress
uniforms fit for the occasion. These included Spock,
McCoy, Scotty, Sulu, and Uhura.

Hox and Ferlein, the bodyguards, were also invited, but they had insisted on standing nearby and
"observing," as Ferlein put it. The two had mostly
stayed in their quarters during the voyage and had
split their time hovering over Hannah wherever
she went. Each time they appeared, however, they
looked noticeably more pasty-faced and sickly. The
immune response had begun with them as well
as with Hannah. Merling, so far, seemed to have
avoided it, perhaps because he was not a Vesbian
native and had had the gene therapy later in life.

Hannah was not less beautiful, but she certainly
was less vibrant, Kirk thought. She was alternately
flush and pale, as if fever were running through her
body. She had begun to tire more easily, but she was
making up for this by sheer force of will. Hannah
had been as ardent as ever with him as before, perhaps more so, sensing her coming illness.

She had dutifully allowed McCoy to examine
her and administer the daily immune-suppressant
vaccine. McCoy had been entrusted with a large
enough supply of the precious material to treat the
Vesbians for a longer mission. The problem was, the

vaccine didn't seem to be working; or, if it was, it seemed to be losing effectiveness.

Kirk's own feelings had not lessened.

At the dinner, Hannah found out about Sulu's interest in ancient firearms and both discovered a particular fascination with blunderbuss pistols of seventeenth-century Earth. Hannah, it seemed, was a crack marksman and had competed in phaser-skeet competitions on Vesbius. Sulu was obviously smitten with Hannah, and Kirk found himself feeling jealousy. But it didn't take Sulu long to see in which direction Hannah's interest lay and, although his kindness to her did not wane, all flirting went out of it.

Dinner was spare by the standards of Vesbius. Kirk did not attempt to equal the feast he'd been given on the colony world, but he did order his personal cache of 2169 Saurian brandy broken out. It had been a gift from a connoisseur, perhaps the greatest of all time, and was the only beverage Kirk knew of that might be the equal of Vesbian ale.

Merling, for his part, behaved tolerably at the dinner. He spoke of the military life on Vesbius, and his role in organizing a planetary militia that he considered second to none.

"I'm not a part of the first wave of settlers, nor am I a native-born child of the planet. No, I am a veteran of the Deneb II expeditionary force," Merling said. "We saw action during the uprising on that benighted world, and I personally commanded a charge on the rebels' position."

"Wasn't that uprising notorious for the use of military nanotechnology?" Scott asked. "Using that stuff is a war crime and forbidden—and for good reason."

"The rebels would stop at nothing," Merling said. "They were animals. I lost a lot of men that day purely from the lack of discipline. It was my own fault. I had been lax on their training, afraid, as a young lieutenant, to push them farther than they wanted to go. It cost some of them their lives. Since that day, I have believed that a strong hand saves lives, and that discipline—of both the self and the body politic—is key."

"Is this why you advocate replacing the Council with a single voice during the crisis and afterward?" Spock asked.

"Yes," Merling answered, without looking at Spock. It sounded like he was spitting out something distasteful in his answer.

"There is a certain logic in your position," said Spock. "During times of war a democratically elected leader becomes less a representative of the people and more a commander-in-chief. Those who do not go into a war organized and acting as one often live to regret this fact. Believers in democracy do not, however, think that the same logic applies to civilian life. There is a certain degree of disorder that is necessary for change and creativity to bring about advancements. Even Vulcans make room for this in our society."

"It may be the Vulcan way, but it should not be the way of Vesbius. We Vesbians are a different breed."

"Indeed," Spock said. "You are. Literally."

"Gentlemen, please let us not argue over this now," said Hannah. "We must come together in this difficult time as best we can. It is my belief that we should use the institutions that we already have in place. On Vesbius, there is the possibility of the chancellor taking a strong hand in emergency conditions, and my father has done just that. Witness the fact that he ordered me on this voyage against my wishes. Even now, I would rather be supervising the shelter reconstruction on Vesbius. But the point remains: Many decisions have been made unilaterally—of necessity. This is one of the reasons the Exos terrorists are dissatisfied and strike out."

"But surely they are a fringe element," said Doctor McCoy, "who are using this situation to advance their own agenda."

"They are," said Hannah. "But we must not dismiss the legitimate dissent just because some choose to take it too far."

"You were in those shelters pulling out bodies," said McCoy, "as was I under the ballroom. If you're truly expressing forgiveness . . ."

"I forgive, Doctor," replied Hannah. "But I do not forget. And I will do everything in my power to prevent it from happening again, including prosecuting those who are found to have participated in this action. And we *will* find them eventually, Doctor. Vesbius is a very small world in some ways."

With that, Kirk raised his glass of Vesbian ale, and the Vesbians, for their part, raised their Saurian brandy, which they'd politely tried and found as good as Kirk had hoped. "To Vesbius," the captain offered. "May there be a bright future for her and her citizens."

"Hear, hear," came the calls of the others. Hannah blushed and raised her glass, as did Merling. They drank.

"This beer *is* extraordinarily good," said Uhura, who had decided to try the Vesbian ale at Hannah's request . "And I usually prefer wine."

"I hoped you would find it so, Lieutenant," said Hannah, with a beaming and genuine smile.

The dinner was a success. Kirk had a replicator specialist create a new linguine recipe that he named Tholian Web. It included herbs and spices from several of the planets that the *Enterprise* had visited over the course of its mission and imparted quite an exotic flavor to the ordinary pasta. At times Hannah seemed lost in thought, and when Kirk asked her what she was thinking about, she answered the she was trying to figure out from aroma and from taste what the herbs were that she was experiencing. It seemed that every aspect of biology was of interest to Vesbians, particularly to Hannah.

The trip out proved to be one of the best of Kirk's life. He allowed his feelings to bloom for Hannah, and she the same. In the confines of the ship and despite the pressure of the mission, it was as if they were living out a long relationship in fast forward.

While Hannah nominally bunked in Uhura's quarters, it was the captain's quarters where she was most often to be found. Her bodyguards had been ordered to make themselves scarce at such times and were usually lurking around the corridors of deck five with scowls on their faces.

"You're the xenobiologist," Kirk said to her. "How can we be so compatible when we're so different?"

They lay together on the deck beside his bunk, having fallen off in the process of making furious love. They were wrapped in one of Kirk's few keepsakes, a vintage blanket from a Federation vessel.

"Biology is a wonderful field of study," Hannah answered. "But a rose is a rose is a rose."

"Fair enough," Kirk said.

"Why does this blanket say *U.S.S. Archer*?" Hannah asked. "We are on the *Enterprise,* after all."

Kirk fingered the worn fabric. "It was my mother's. She wrapped me in it once."

"And thereby hangs a tale?"

"Thereby hangs a tale," Kirk said. "But what about you?"

"I grew up in the country. My parents were biologists who became farmers." Hannah sat up, a leg held against her chest.

"And they grew you."

"In a manner of speaking," Hannah said. "I studied biology. And that led to anthropology. And economics. And politics." She shook her hair and it fell around her shoulders and over her breasts in unkempt but beautiful waves. "So here I am."

"A politician?"

"Yes. And still a farm girl in many ways."

"But your father is the chancellor of Vesbius, not a farmer."

"And who do you think got him elected?"

Kirk sat up beside Hannah, put a hand on her chin, and kissed her softly. "You?" he said.

"Little old me. I managed the campaign."

"The power behind the throne."

"We don't have a throne on Vesbius," said Hannah. "We are a democracy, and I aim to keep it that way." She took his hand in hers and squeezed it. He could feel the tension within her, and the resolve. "Even through all this." And then she let out a long breath and released it, and the tension within her seemed to dissolve.

"You think I have it pretty easy, just having

a starship to run, don't you?" Kirk said with a laugh.

She leaned over and brushed her lips against his cheek. "I would never say that, Jim."

"But you might think it."

"If I ever did, I'd keep it to myself," Hannah replied.

"You are a politician, aren't you?" Kirk said.

"I'm also a woman," she said. She took him by the shoulders, pushing him gently toward the blanket. "A woman in love with you." She was quiet for a moment, then finally spoke with a twinkle in her eye. "It doesn't take much to see that the problems of two little people don't amount to a hill of beans in this crazy world."

"Someday you'll understand that," Kirk said, completing the quote. "*Casablanca*?"

"*Casablanca*," she said. "Crazy ending. Sad. Kiss me."

He kissed her and they came together again. And when it was over and Kirk was sure she lay sleeping on the blanket, he allowed himself to say the words: "I love you, Hannah." Then he kissed her a final time and lay down beside her.

Hannah did not open her eyes, but she smiled.

"Here's looking at you, kid," she whispered.

Two days later, they arrived at the Janus VI system. They had notified the mining colony that they were on their way. Kirk had not communicated what their purpose was because he did not know the state of affairs between the miners and the Horta. He suspected it was cordial, since the mine was still putting out a record haul of pergium each quarter. But he did not want anyone to do his talking for him. This was going to be difficult without prejudices being formed beforehand.

There was a new mining director, Debra Weisskopf, a big, blustery woman who seemed a hale and hearty sort. She immediately greeted Kirk and his landing party with a strong handshake that almost crushed Kirk's fingers. She had flaming red hair, and Scotty, whom Kirk brought down with him, was clearly smitten with her.

"What a woman," Kirk heard Scotty mutter under his breath after the handshake.

Kirk, Hannah, and Merling sat down in chairs in front of the director's desk. The others in the landing party—Spock, Scotty, McCoy, and the two Vesbian bodyguards, Hox and Ferlein—were crowded into the small office.

Weisskopf did not stay behind her desk but instead plopped herself down on its surface, facing them. Informality seemed to be part of her leadership style, but Kirk noticed a series of carefully drawn charts that decorated her office walls, and all of the trends on the charts were pointing up. "All right, now we can solve the big mystery of why the *Enterprise* is back at Janus VI?" Laughing, she added, "I know it is not for shore leave." It was such a contagious laugh that everyone else, except Spock, joined in with her.

"Perhaps some other time," Kirk replied. "What we want, Director Weisskopf—"

"Call me Debra."

"What we're here for, Debra, is the Horta. We want to talk with them, and, quite frankly, we want to recruit some of them to come with us."

Now Weisskopf's laugh was even louder and more raucous, but this time the others did not join in with it. She was laughing at them. "You've got to be kidding," she said. "Those Horta are very attached to this world and to their rock. And what do you want them for, may I ask? Are you going to make them into Starfleet cadets?"

"That might not be a bad idea at some point," noted Spock.

"But that is not our purpose at present," said Kirk. "We need their help to break apart an asteroid that is on a collision course with the planet Vesbius, whose representatives have accompanied us, Ambassador Hannah Faber and Major Johan Merling."

"You want them to . . . do *what*, exactly?"

"To cut the asteroid as a jeweler might cut a gem," Spock explained. "That is the closest analogy that I can think of at present."

The mining director nodded her head. She

considered what she'd heard for a moment and then her nodding became a more enthusiastic head bobbing. The director was nothing if not enthusiastic. "Yes, yes, that is a very interesting idea, and something the Horta might consider if there were something in it for them."

"Something in it for them?" said Spock, with a trace of disbelief in his voice. "When I communicated with the Horta All Mother previously, there was no indication that she would require *quid pro quo* to make an agreement."

"That's the All Mother," said Weisskopf. "The children are another matter entirely. As you know, we established a primitive method of communicating with the Horta. We have a wigwag movement code worked out, a system of colored-stone exchange, and, when all else fails, we leave messages to one another carved into rocks with either phaser or poured acid. We put in a request for a telepath or an empath, but no luck. In any case, I have found the kids to be not only intelligent and hardworking, they also rather enjoy making a profit."

"A profit?" said Kirk. "That implies they have something to do with their money."

"It does indeed," answered Weisskopf.

"And what exactly does a Horta *do* with credits?" asked McCoy. "I don't suppose they spend it on gambling and wild women?"

"Well, you might be surprised. You're closer

than you think," Weisskopf answered. "One thing they do is collect rocks. Geological specimens from throughout the galaxy. Things that can't be found here in the mine. They're particularly fond of silicon geodes from Earth."

"Do they . . . study them?" asked Kirk.

The director laughed. "Heck no. They consider them a delicacy. They *eat* them, of course."

"Of course," Kirk replied.

The journey into the depths of the mine was a long one on the carrier sled, and Spock used the time to consider the reactions of those about him. For the humans among them, the descent must have seemed eerie. The mine lighting system could only dispel some of the pitch-blackness of the place, and the sameness of the walls and ceiling could make the visitor feel utterly lost. Miners who were intimately familiar with passageways might be able to find their way back; for anyone else it would be a challenge.

The Vulcan found the convoluted mines interesting. While he would never feel at home in such close confines, he did not experience the claustrophobia that the humans seemed to be experiencing. Spock did not entirely understand this emotion-laden sensation. After all, a body could only fit where there was sufficient space in a passageway.

If a person estimated where he or she might fit and then got stuck, he or she could either call for help or resign him- or herself to fate. Thrashing about and growing restive would not change things one iota.

Nevertheless, the caves did present a problem. Spock was tall, and the Horta were no more than waist height to him. The captain merely had to stoop a bit to make his way. Spock often found himself bent over double in the Horta-carved caves and shuffling along in a most unpleasant manner. An Earthman might have called it a "duck walk."

The miners who were guiding them did not seem to feel the same trepidation about the size of the tunnels. In fact, the miners seemed to be in a better humor the closer they got to the Horta living area.

"Those baby Horta are kind of frisky," said Director Weisskopf, who accompanied them. "But they're basically goodhearted creatures. And smarter than the devil. Only—"

"Only what?" asked Kirk

"Do not treat them like animals. They're not animals; they're reasoning beings, just like you and I—only they are young."

"Yes, about two and a half Earth years old at this point," said Spock.

The director explained: "They have something like a group mind, like bees or ant colonies, although each one is much more individual than a bee. They've learned a great deal in the past two years. Each Horta seems to know what the others know. They act pretty much like adolescents."

"Teenagers?" said Kirk.

"Yes. Emotionally, with a teenage hive mind, too."

Kirk turned to Spock. "Maybe we can use that, Spock."

The passageway they had been scuttling along gave way to a large chamber. This was the former egg chamber. But now it had been transformed into living quarters, a vast apartment complex, the walls decorated with glittering minerals, quartz, and feldspar. Mica windows glinted between individual stalls, which appeared to be living spaces. And the chamber was no longer filled with eggs. The eggs were gone; now it was filled with hundreds of hatchlings. Perhaps thousands. And each as large as a reclining couch.

"Fascinating," said Spock.

"My, how they've grown," Kirk quipped.

They were about the same size as the All Mother. But not all of them were the same reddish brown hue. Some shone with a blue or greenish tint, and it took Kirk a moment to realize that this must be decoration of some sort.

"Clothing," Spock offered.

"Spock ?" asked Kirk.

"The Horta appear to have the same drive to adorn their bodies as do other sentient life forms. Even though they are silicon based and their internal structure does not correspond to any aliens we have encountered before. I wonder what the various rocks and colorations with which they adorn themselves mean. It would be a fascinating study."

"Agreed, but that will have to wait," said Kirk. "Let's try to establish communication." He turned to the director. "Can you tell them that we are about to attempt to establish a direct line of mental communication between one of them and Mister Spock?"

"I'll try," said the director. "I would suggest that you start off with Slider Dan over there." She pointed toward a Horta who had drawn close to them when they had entered the chamber. "That's not his real name, of course, just what we call him. I suppose because of the way he moves through the rock. The Horta respect him, too. He's not their leader exactly—he's the one that understands humans—so we usually use him as our interpreter. For a Horta he seems to have a pretty good grasp of human nature."

"I hope he gets along well with Vulcans, too," said Kirk. "But I suppose that's the best place to start. How do you know it's a he, anyway?"

"Oh, they have . . . characteristics," said the director. "Extendable bumps that we're pretty sure are ovipositors on females and penises on the male.

You can tell male from the female by . . . well, you can't really tell easily unless you're used to it, and the Horta wants to show its underside. Just trust me, that Horta is a male."

The director took out a handheld device that Spock was about to inquire about when she pulled the trigger on the device and a large sonic signal reverberated through the chamber. It was similar to a rescue air horn in quality and intensity. Then from a side pack of items she carried at her waist, the director took out several different colored round stones.

"They communicate with marbles," said Kirk.

"Marbles?" said Spock.

"An ancient Earth pastime," Kirk replied. "A children's game using smooth stones, like ball bearings. The object is to knock the player's stones out of an area, and then you get to keep them."

"Sounds rather barbaric," said Spock.

"Oh, it is," said Kirk, "but entertaining."

The director put the marbles in front of the Horta named Slider Dan. True to his name, he slid over the stones with a rumble. Spock noted that the marbles had various colors, and the director had placed them in a specified order. With a few more examples, Spock was confident he could understand the code and read the marbles when they were laid down. But it seemed a very cumbersome method to communicate complicated ideas—and what he had to communicate was very complicated indeed.

The male Horta withdrew from the marbles. The mining director looked down and checked the order.

"Well," said Weisskopf. "He says he's game for discussion."

"And you explained to him what we're proposing to do?" asked Kirk.

"I told them that this one"—she pointed to Spock—"wished to speak with him by touching him. I don't think he knows what that means any more than I do, really. But he said yes. You want me to ask him again? In some other way?"

"I believe that will be sufficient, Captain," said Spock. "After all, no one is ever really prepared for a Vulcan mind probe."

The Vulcan approached the Horta and knelt down beside it. He could smell the sulfuric tinge of its acidic flesh, but he knew from his previous contact with the All Mother that most of the acid was generated and held underneath the creature. The carapace of a Horta was not toxic or harmful. Contact would be necessary for the mind meld to truly be effective.

Spock reached out and touched the Horta. It seemed to flinch, and it drew back a shuffle step, but then it remained still and allowed him to continue positioning his hands on its surface.

Spock sent tenuous mental inquiries directed toward the Horta. Like many beings that had not experienced telepathic communication with alien species, there was the initial recoil, and a moment of fright. But this Horta appeared to be rather perceptive and seemed to grasp quickly what was going on. In fact, it—he—seemed to know exactly who Spock was.

You are the Vulcan who touched the All Mother's mind. It was the Horta Slider Dan, his thoughts sifting into Spock's mind. *You are the communicator who found a way to save the children. I am honored to be in contact with you, sir. We have among us a semi-telepathic bond, and when you speak with me you are speaking to many, although what is communicated is more feeling than intelligent thought.*

Spock replied in thought; *I am pleased that we may communicate together, and be as one for a short time. The procedure requires that you open your mind to me and I to you. It is more than mere speech; it is a complete sharing of being. Will you let me do this, and will you engage with me?*

I shall, Spock. This is not so different from our normal meeting communications, the Horta replied. *You understand that we "talk" with smells and psionic waves that allow us to form a clan mind and the hive mind. It works best among family members, but all of us are capable of some form of mental communication with one another.*

Thank you. And with that, Spock entered into full mind meld with the Horta.

What he encountered there first were thoughts of rock. The jagged form of the mineral trace, the crack that might be exploited to open up new territory. The weight of the planet above, and the heat of the planet below. The beauty of vast caves and minerals deep under the surface hidden where no human could survive or enter—but those places were the playground of the Horta. The chemical tang, the smell of minerals and salts. And the delightful taste of those minerals that trade with the humans provided, especially those delicious geodes so enjoyed by Slider Dan—the meaning of whose name was not so far off from the human approximation, although his true name was an unpronounceable amalgamation of images, of a fast and swift youthful Horta passing through rock as a swimmer might slice through water.

I am named for a mythological hero in our distant past, Spock. Now that their thoughts were one, Spock instantly understood the myth from which the name derived. The process of comprehension was rather like a computer download. It was a sort of tall tale, and Slider Dan was immensely proud of his name, which was unique to his Horta clan.

"Spock" is an ancient name on Vulcan. I believe my human mother gave it to me so that I might better fit in.

You Vulcans have heaviness about you that I think the All Mother would appreciate. But what do you do for fun on Vulcan?

Fun? We reason.

Oh.

We occasionally engage in competitions of logic. I myself enjoy a good game of three-dimensional chess with the captain.

Sounds delightful.

Spock could not tell whether or not the Horta was being genuine or was making a joke at his expense. It seemed a mind meld still allowed wiggle room with the truth. In any case, it didn't matter, as Spock was not offended. The time had come to communicate his mission.

Using the mind meld, Spock quickly explained what it was that Starfleet Command and the Vesbians wished from the Horta.

After he was finished, but before the mind meld was broken, Spock felt the Horta draw away from his mind as if to shield a thought he did not wish to communicate. And then there was full contact yet again.

We wish to discuss, and ruminate among ourselves. We must consider. It is a large thing you ask of us, to leave this world even for a short time. None of us has departed ever. In fact, if we go on to the surface, some of us experience a thing very similar to what the humans experience in very tight spaces.

We will have to overcome this if we are to accompany you. Let us withdraw now, and I will give you an answer in a little while. Thank you so much for visiting us again, and speaking in such a manner to us. You are greatly honored among our people. We have a name for you, a special name.

And what is that? Spock asked

Speaker from the Stars, thought the Horta. And then Spock and Slider Dan broke contact. Spock stepped back, dazed for a moment, as he usually was, after an intense mind meld.

"Spock," said Kirk, "are you all right?"

"Perfectly," answered Spock after a moment. "I have communicated our purpose to the Horta. They wish time to consider it and will return with a response shortly."

"I hope it's *very* shortly," said Kirk. "Time is one thing we don't have very much of."

"I believe the Horta understand this as well," answered Spock.

Five minutes later, Slider Dan inched toward Spock and signaled, with the bright glow on his carapace that resembled the flow of magma underneath a rocky crust , that he was ready to reestablish the mind meld. When Spock did so, there was only one sentence communicated.

We wish to show you something, and we wish to ask you a question.

Come with you? Where?

To the place that only Speaker from the Stars may know. The other humans will have to remain. Only you may accompany us to this place.

I will need to consult with my captain, answered Spock.

Of course, replied the Horta.

Spock pulled back from the mind meld long enough to address Kirk. "Captain, Slider Dan wishes me to accompany him deeper under the planet surface. Furthermore, he does not wish anyone but me to come along with him."

Kirk did not look pleased.

"Spock, do you sense any danger?"

"I do not," Spock answered. "I believe he wants to show me something important to the Horta, and doing so may further our mission."

"All right," Kirk said. "Go. But be careful, Spock."

"Understood, Captain."

Spock wondered if his following the Horta away might seem a bit zombie-like to those who were watching. While he was aware of what his body was doing, he was distracted by maintaining the link and could not achieve a fluid physical motion. Spock walked after the Horta into one of the tunnel entrances. It seemed a random tunnel, not unlike the other ones, but he knew from the Horta's thoughts that this was a special passageway that led somewhere important, somewhere no man had gone before.

After he had entered the top tunnel and walked ninety-one meters, Spock turned to get a glimpse of where he had come from. A group of Horta had moved in behind them and, to Spock's puzzlement, they closed the tunnel up entirely, forming it back into solid rock. He would not be coming back this way.

You will now need to leave your communicator here in the tunnel, said Slider Dan. *We know this device might be traced, and we do not wish to reveal where we are taking you.*

Very well, Spock answered. He dropped his communicator and followed the Horta onward, into the darkness.

Eight

Captain's log, Stardate 6408.6. On the mining outpost of Janus VI, Mister Spock, after having mind melded with the Horta, has disappeared into a tunnel of the planetoid. I expected Spock to return shortly, but he has been gone for over two hours. Meanwhile, the Vesbian ambassadors and I have been waiting for word. Time is not on our side. With no sign of Spock, I have determined to venture into the depths to seek him out. If the operation to save Vesbius is to succeed, we must be on our way soon. If we do not, it won't matter whether we are able to recruit the Horta's help. The colony will be doomed.

Kirk paced around the Horta egg chamber in consternation. After Spock had stepped into the tunnel, the Horta had begun to retreat from the area. Several dozen of them went down the tunnel after Spock and then suddenly its entrance had been closed. This surprised Kirk, and it seemed ominous. Spock had followed the Horta peacefully, but the captain had to ask himself now how much of that had been Spock and how much might have been the effect of being submerged in a group mind. There was no way he would be able to find Spock unaided. They could only hope to be able to trace his communicator.

Five minutes passed. Ten, then twenty. Still no Spock. Then, as if on cue, the remainder of the Horta—hundreds of them—began to leave the room. At first this was in dribs and drabs, and finally it became a mass exodus. They left through every tunnel available, and within a half hour, the only beings that were in the room were the humans.

"I've never seen *that* before," said Weisskopf. "They sure seem restive."

Kirk agreed. He opened his communicator. "*Enterprise,* this is Kirk. Get Sulu and Chekov beamed down here immediately with a tricorder." Kirk considered. Was this an act of aggression? A misunderstanding? He fervently hoped that it was the latter. "Scotty, can you lock on to this signal?"

"Maximum range, sir, but we have a good lock. But if you go any farther under that rock, you'll be out of transporter range."

"Understood. Tell them to arrive unarmed," Kirk said. He hoped he was making the right decision. For Spock's sake, and the sake of Vesbius. "Lock on to our four Vesbians."

Hannah had come along with them, as had Merling, but Kirk did not want to take them with him when he went to search for Spock. Merling had obviously disliked the Horta on sight. He wouldn't be useful. Hannah had not fared well on the descent and was clearly in some pain. Her face was drawn and she looked feverish.

"I want the entire Vesbius party back on the ship," Kirk said. "I have to look for Spock, and having you along will slow me down."

Merling nodded. He was obviously quite content to get out of the confines of the mine and away from the Horta.

Hannah turned to Kirk with fire in her eyes.

"But I must go with you, Jim," she said to him. "This is the reason you brought me here." She turned to the bodyguards, Hox and Ferlein. "They will return." She addressed them with a smile: "I do not think there is much you can do to protect me in this situation."

Hox seemed disturbed by his surroundings, and he quickly agreed. He was ready to go. But Ferlein protested. "I have direct orders from your father, Chief Advisor."

"To guard me from the factions of Vesbius," said Hannah. "That has always been your mandate. Not to accompany me into tunnels looking for aliens. Besides, you are obviously suffering from the separation sickness."

"We're both natives, ma'am," said Ferlein. "You know it's going to strike you as well, and soon. I demand that you let me do my job. Your father will kill me if I let you—"

"Simon, I order you to go back to the ship," Hannah said.

"No, I will not," he said. "I will stay with you! It's my duty to you and your father after the good you did for my family, you must—"

The strain was too much. The man fainted. Kirk and Hannah moved to catch him before he hit the cavern floor. Kirk motioned to Hox and Merling to come over and help. The other men had been watching with morbid fascination. Hox obviously wanted to get the hell out of this place.

Hox took Hannah's place and held the other bodyguard under the shoulder, and Kirk allowed Merling to take his load. After a moment, Ferlein came to and tried to stand. He groggily looked up at Hannah. "Must come . . . with . . . duty . . ."

"You are going to bed," Hannah said. She looked to Merling and Hox. "Get him to Doctor McCoy, please."

"Of course, Chief Advisor," said Merling. "The sooner we can get him away from these lifeless halls, the better."

Hannah turned to Kirk. "I'm coming with you, Jim."

"And what if your own rejection sickness suddenly strikes? What am I to do with you?"

"The immunosuppressant vaccine is working for the moment," she replied. "I'll be all right, Captain."

Kirk nodded, but he wasn't nearly as sure about this as Hannah seemed to be. Nevertheless, she had a point. She was the emissary from a world in distress. This was the reason she'd journeyed to Janus VI, to personally ask for help for her people.

That Kirk worried that he might be harming Hannah should not have been part of his decision. She had grown weaker by the day, and Ferlein's collapse had alarmed him. The rejection sickness seemed to come on quickly and was completely debilitating.

He could order her beamed aboard. One word to Scotty, and there would be little she could do about it.

Except hate him forever for treating her like a child.

No, this was her decision.

"All right," he said, and he flipped open his communicator. Kirk modified his transport order. Merling, Hox and the still groggy Ferlein dematerialized, to be quickly replaced by Sulu and Chekov.

The captain led the search party, which also included two expert miners Director Weisskopf had insisted accompany them, down into the depths after the Horta. Each was issued a hover light, a small but powerful personal headlamp that got its name from the way it hovered just off the shoulder and keyed off eye movement to cast a diode-generated light in a useful direction.

Kirk's instinct told him to avoid all side tunnels and to go as deep as possible. The miners brought along phosphorescent markers that allowed them to blaze the trail back should the search party become disoriented or lost, and they were busy marking the walls as the party descended. The problem was, it wasn't always obvious which paths would lead deeper.

Chekov solved the problem by using his tricorder to ping the rock with sonic sensors and detect the best route. After a while, the side tunnels gave out, and it was obvious which way to go. They were deeper into the planetary crust of Janus VI than any human had ever been before.

Down and down they went. After what seemed an age of continuous stooped-over walking, the tunnel they were in grew larger. There were fresh signs—pointed out by the miners, who knew what to look for—that the Horta had recently passed this way. The miners were as confused as Kirk about the lack of Horta in the vicinity. They had never experienced a complete withdrawal of the Horta clans before this.

"They been underfoot since I came out to this rock to work," said one. "Used to irritate me you couldn't get away from a Horta. Now I kind of miss the buggers. Tunnels are lonely without 'em."

And then the passageway in which they were traveling led out into a larger chamber—and there were Horta here. These were not normal-sized Horta, but smaller, about the size of large dogs. They were arrayed against the wall opposite Kirk and the search party, and they seemed to be blocking the only visible exit to the chamber.

"These Horta seem somehow . . . friendly," said Sulu.

"Are they a variant species? Some kind of specialized caste?"

"Never seen anything like them before," one of the miners answered.

"Captain, my readings on these Horta correlate with what we have in the xenobiology database," said Chekov, gazing down at his tricorder readout. "They have the same internal structure, only smaller, sir. The same . . . everything. I believe this is the exact same species, sir."

"It's a nursery," said Hannah. "Or a daycare center."

Kirk nodded slowly. "Could be. Maybe they don't all mature at the same rate. Maybe some eggs hatched later than others."

"Baby Horta," said Sulu. "Cute."

"You may be right," said Kirk. "But these children are blocking the entrance to that tunnel on the opposite side of the chamber. Let's get through them."

Kirk walked in the direction of the line of small Horta. When he got to them, they did not move, and he stopped the party's forward motion.

"We have to get past you," he said to them, knowing the futility of saying it.

Kirk looked over the crowd of little ones. They weren't exactly side-by-side. If he turned sideways, he might be able to shuffle through them.

"All right, stay here," he told the team, and he made the move to go forward himself. After his first couple of steps, the crowd of small Horta parted and formed a gap for Kirk. As he walked forward, so did the gap. Hannah followed behind him and she was also allowed through. But when Sulu tried it, the Horta would not budge. The same for Chekov and the others.

"I guess they just want us to pass," Kirk called back to the stranded party. "Wait here. Mister Sulu, you're in charge. If we're not back in an hour, use whatever means you can to get past these . . . kindergartners . . . and come looking for us."

"Aye, Captain," said Sulu. "Be careful."

"I don't think they want to hurt us," Kirk said. "But they do seem to be picky about whom they want to deal with at the moment. I don't know if that's a good or a bad thing. But you have your orders."

With that Kirk turned and entered into the exit tunnel of the nursery chamber (if that's what the cavern was). Hannah Faber was behind him.

Kirk allowed the baby Horta to shuffle along with him as he walked deeper and even farther down into the depths of Janus VI. And, as with the last chamber, the tunnel began to widen out and to gain a higher and higher ceiling until Kirk found himself walking into a vast cathedral of rock. Light was provided by magma flow that shot through the rock surface in tiny veins. It gave a beautiful, eerie, reddish caste to the chamber. Kirk and Hannah turned off their hover lights. The temperature inside the chamber was quite hot and Kirk was sweating, but the heat wasn't intolerable to humans, at least not yet.

There were more Horta. Big and small. Horta were everywhere, filling every nook and cranny on the sides of the rocky cathedral.

Ahead of him across the chamber, Kirk saw a blue speck. As he drew closer, dodging around boulders and following the very smooth, winding path through the center of the chamber, the blue dot became the blue of Spock's science officer's uniform shirt. Closer still, and there was Spock standing, waiting for him to arrive.

"Greetings, Captain. Greetings, Chief Advisor Faber," Spock called out. "Welcome to the Great Chamber of the Horta."

"Spock, report," Kirk said as soon as he was within speaking distance of his first officer. He and Hannah came to join Spock on a rise that revealed crowds of even more Horta in the back half of the cavern.

"I have received a most interesting proposition, Captain," said Spock. "But before I go into that, I would like to reintroduce you to a Horta you have met before."

Spock led them to a corner of the chamber where, against a crystalline stalactite, a creature rested. It was smoother and less bumpy than the other Horta.

Like stone that has served as a walkway for centuries, Kirk thought. *Worn smooth.*

Hannah, who had pressed close to Kirk and wore a tense expression on her face, now smiled at the sight.

"This is she, isn't it? This is the All Mother," Hannah said.

"Very perceptive, Chief Advisor," said Spock. "This is indeed the All Mother, and this chamber has been constructed by the Horta as the final resting place for her. It is a place of honor and reflection for the Horta."

"What's this all about, Spock?" asked Kirk. "I presume you've gotten to the bottom of it."

"Both literally and metaphorically," answered Spock. "This chamber is as low as the Horta have delved. I have been locked in a continuous mind meld with the Horta since I left the chamber above. In fact, they are considerably adept at such communication, and they have not released me from the meld. I have not attempted to forcefully break it as of yet."

"Isn't that dangerous for you, Spock? You might lose yourself in such a situation."

"It is a risk," said Spock. "But the Horta seem excited by communicating with an older person and they will not stop asking me questions—questions which I feel obliged to answer. They are asking things such as 'Why is the sky orange?' and 'Why do we have to die?' Things of that nature. On Vulcan, such questions are not taken lightly."

"Sounds like you're in a mind meld with a bunch of eager, inquisitive kids," said Kirk.

"That is exactly what is happening," Spock answered. "They do not wish to harm me, but they keep wishing to ask one last question."

"Still, hours of mind meld can't be good for your own sanity, can it?"

"I believe I have determined a way to break myself free," Spock said. "But to do so at this point might harm the Horta, and I am not willing to do that. They are remarkably clever, and there is great wisdom in their cultural philosophy, but these Horta are, for all intents and purposes, adolescent in their mentality."

"Don't want to take candy from babies, Spock?" said Kirk.

"I beg your pardon, Captain?"

Kirk smiled. "Never mind."

"Are they individuals at all, or some kind of hive, like the cloud-dusters of Warburton's World?" asked Hannah.

"Both, Chief Advisor," said Spock. "They are a hive mind of sorts, but this seems to be a stage on their way to further development into individuals. I have communicated extensively with the All Mother on this matter."

"And what does the All Mother have to say?" asked Kirk.

"She apologizes for the impetuousness of her children, for one thing," said Spock. "And she wishes us to indulge her by listening to their request."

"Listening, how?"

"Through me," said Spock. "That is the only way she can adequately express herself, she believes."

"Very well. What is this request?" asked Kirk.

"The All Mother is in decline. She is in rapid decline for one of her species and will die within a standard year. She explains that she *should* have died earlier."

"Should have?"

"Her children have been very resourceful," Spock answered. "They have maintained her past the normal cycle. In any case, her death will not be unusual, but in the natural course of things concerning Horta. She is a specialized being, and only one of her is born in a generation. As soon as her

work is done—that is, bringing forth a new generation of Horta—her biology shuts down."

"Why is she still alive, then?"

"The mine supervisor is incorrect in her assessment when she claims that the Horta merely wish
to consume, and that that is why they engage in
trade for the Horta equivalent of delicacies. They
are also engaged in keeping the All Mother alive by
feeding her exotic minerals from off planet, minerals they know will sustain her, keep her hormone-
equivalent systems recharged. This is where the vast
majority of the Horta share of the mine's take goes.
The geodes from Earth and various minerals from
other planets act as a sort of vitamin supplement for
the All Mother."

"So they're keeping her alive . . . against her
wishes?"

"Not precisely, Captain," Spock replied. "She is
a most caring and indulgent mother, and she has
allowed them to maintain their sentimental attachment to her out of love. She believes two and a half
standard years is enough time to see them settled,
however, and now it is time for her to fade away and
to send her children forth."

"All right," Kirk said. "I understand."

"But here is where the request comes in, Captain," said Spock. "The Horta venerate the All
Mother and they want someone to take her place."

"So . . . one of them can become the new leader?"

"It is not that simple, Captain. In the normal course of things, the All Mother will die and the Horta will carry on, but without the All Mother to combine them into a full hive mind. The hive mind is necessary for rapid group learning at first—this is why the Horta of Janus VI seem to have learned so quickly and been able to take on responsibilities in the mines. It is an efficient way to deal with adolescence and cognitive development, although it does tend to limit individual initiative except in a few extraordinary individuals."

"Sounds like human teenagers in school," muttered Kirk.

Spock ignored the comment. "After the All Mother dies, the Horta become full individuals. Although telepathic contact is still possible, especially along Horta clan lines, the hive mind is broken, and the Horta are faced with being alone within their own minds for much of the time."

"Like us," Kirk said.

"Precisely, Captain," Spock answered. "The Horta have observed humans, and these Horta have decided they wish to avoid the loneliness. They do not wish the All Mother to die. And failing that, they want a new All Mother who can maintain the larger hive mind. What they wish for cannot be, however. This is not physiologically possible within the species. A new All Mother can only be bred once in a generation, and her birth triggers the death of the species, but for their eggs."

"So these new Horta are faced with a dilemma," Hannah said. "A wonderful childhood they do not wish to leave, but a mother who can't stay."

"Yes, quite correct. The All Mother believes that perpetual adolescence will not be good for the Horta," Spock said.

The surface of the All Mother began to glow as if in agitation. Spock reached over and touched her, and when he did, his voice changed to a sonorous monotone as he took on the persona of the rock creature that spoke through him. "Like many children who do not wish to leave or lose their parents, my children are not ready for my passing. They believe they have hit upon another solution, and, because I'm an indulgent mother, I have heard them out. I would also beg you to hear them out, Captain."

Kirk put his hands out toward the All Mother Horta in greeting and understanding, even though the words he heard came from Spock. "Of course," he said. "It would seem that children are the same everywhere."

The Horta released a small puff of sulfuric steam that Kirk hoped was laughter.

Spock broke contact and took a step back from the All Mother. "What the Horta want," says Spock, "is to have *me* become the new All Mother."

"*You*, Spock?" said Kirk. "Somebody's mom?"

"It is an unlikely proposition," said Spock. "But I believe what the All Mother is suggesting is that we play along with them for now. In the end, I think it extremely unlikely that I will be what these young Horta are looking for, and they will recognize that."

Hannah, standing beside Kirk, laughed. The sound brought a moment of lightness to the otherwise eerie situation. "I think Mister Spock might make a fine mother," she said.

"Do you indeed?" said Spock. "I would have much to learn, and the prospect is fascinating, but I fear I would make for a disappointing All Mother."

"And why is that?" Hannah asked.

"Because, Chief Advisor, the Horta, while logical in most ways, are also a very passionate and emotional species," Spock replied. "I believe they will find my Vulcan mindset to be frustrating and ultimately stifling to their development. The All Mother agrees with me."

Again Spock's voice changed, and Kirk understood it was the All Mother speaking through him. "It is time to kick these hatchlings from the nest."

Kirk looked around. The vast chamber was filled with hordes of Horta. They all seemed to be lost in rapt attention focused on the central tableau of Spock and the All Mother, as if waiting in agitated suspense to find out if a parent would grant a request.

Hannah touched Kirk's arm. "They need to hear an answer from you," she said. "Someone outside the hive mind who represents authority."

"I have no authority here," Kirk said.

"You have what they want," Hannah answered. "Spock."

"I can't give them Spock," Kirk said. "It doesn't work that way."

"Of course not," Hannah said. "Not any more than you would give a teenager a new antigrav sled and carte blanche to use it. But you might be able to let them *borrow* the code key to that antigrav sled for a time, let them take it for a spin, and see how they like it."

"Spock is not an antigrav sled," Kirk muttered.

"No, he's not," Hannah replied. "I have helped lead my planet and have made choices in the past few weeks that I never thought to face. But I do believe that a certain ability to go with the flow is sometimes in order."

"Are you suggesting that I *use* the Horta, then yank Spock away from them?"

"I'm suggesting that the situation may work itself out, and in the meantime, my people *need* the cooperation of the Horta. Desperately."

"She speaks the truth," said Spock in his All Mother tone. "It is a gamble. But what in life is not a gamble? My children need to grow up. They have been clever in keeping me alive, but they must release me of their own accord and allow me to reach a respectable ending. I believe this will be a transition to that time, and it will make of my children a very resilient generation. It is clear they are already an extremely clever and resourceful one, and for that I am proud."

Kirk turned and looked over the Horta in the vast chamber. A gamble, the All Mother said. And Spock in the balance, for if a promise was made, the Vulcan *would* find a way of keeping it. As would Kirk. It was a matter of what form that promise might take.

"All right, Spock, ready to translate?"

"Ready, Captain."

Kirk turned and spoke, addressing the entire chamber, although he made sure that he was facing Spock so the Vulcan could hear him, since the communication channel with the Horta lay through Spock.

"I am Captain James T. Kirk of the Federation *Starship Enterprise*. We have decided to accept your terms."

Spock raised an eyebrow in surprise. Kirk shot him a suppressed smile and continued. "Now, here are *my* terms. I will require a contingent of your best diggers. We will travel far away to a new rock that must be carefully dug to save an entire planet from destruction. This work will be difficult and must be done quickly and precisely. Only your best effort will do. As a reward for this, I accept your terms, and I will allow Spock to remain as your new All Mother, with one proviso: that you still desire him to do so at the end of your assignment."

Kirk continued: "You may not desire this when you're done with your task. You are quite young, with great potential and vigor, but little experience of the world beyond these tunnels. Your All Mother agrees with me, I believe, and I'm sure she has said as much to you as well. It is the belief of myself and your All Mother that when you experience the galaxy full of elements, energies, minerals, and molecules out there—and all sorts of things you never imagined—that many of you will want to go further and explore. Find your place among the stars.

"This we can offer you as payment for your services, and I want you to consider it. When the task is done, those are the choices you will have.

"Now, I ask you to release Spock and allow him to return to his duties aboard the *Enterprise* for the duration of this mission.

"When you have selected those who will accompany us, we will begin the process of beaming those Horta aboard the starship. Remember, the materials that our ship is made of are not unlike those that the humans here on Janus VI employ. You are fully capable of cutting through everything in your path. You must be careful not to cut your way out into space when you arrive."

Kirk turned to Hannah. "Have anything to add?"

"Only this." She turned toward Spock and spoke up as Kirk had done. "I and my people will be eternally grateful should you come to our aid. You will have a strong and faithful ally in us ever after. This I promise as the representative of my poor, threatened planet."

"Well done," Kirk said with a smile. He continued his address to the Horta: "You have heard her. Now I challenge you to take on this task and save a world. I believe that this generation of Horta will go down in your history as one of the greatest should we succeed, and that it is one of the toughest and most daring generations, no matter what the outcome. Now please show your assent by releasing my first officer from the hive mind."

There was a general shuffling among the Horta as Kirk finished his speech. And then slowly the shuffling became a clacking, and the clacking became a raucous din, as of a thousand drums beating in rhythm. After that, a loud whistle began to emerge, as if steam were escaping from a thousand vents at once. Kirk, Spock, and Hannah covered their ears to avoid being overcome by the volume. After it had died down, Kirk asked, "So what was that about, Spock?"

"That, Captain, was Horta applause," Spock replied. "Furthermore, they have released me. They have agreed to your terms."

Nine

Spock was back at the science station on the bridge and Kirk was in the captain's chair. Sulu and Chekov were at their customary stations at helm and navigation. What was unusual was in the shuttle bay of the *Enterprise*: five hundred adolescent Horta who were making their first journey to the stars after having been beamed aboard in groups over the course of several hours.

The science officer had been in the shuttle bay to make sure that they were comfortable in their temporary quarters. He reported that the Horta were quite content with the arrangements that had been made. It was, in essence, a large cave much like those to which they were accustomed. The observation deck windows above the flight deck were made opaque in deference to the guests. The crew was asked to respect the Horta's privacy. Light levels were lowered, and infrared fixtures had been installed. The Horta had poor eyesight—Kirk still wasn't sure where on the Horta the eyes *were*—but what vision they had was mostly in the infrared spectrum.

"All right, Ensign Chekov, lay in a course for Vesbius," said Kirk.

Chekov's hand moved over his panel, activating the control interfaces and four-dimensional directional toggles. "Course laid in and ready, Captain."

"Mister Sulu, take us back to Vesbius at warp factor eight." Kirk let out a breath and sat back in his chair. As he sometimes did in the midst of executing a plan, the captain took a moment to evaluate his current course of action. The *Enterprise* was ferrying the Horta across interstellar space, so they could tunnel an asteroid; in his gut the captain knew this was the right decision. Instinct was an indefinable concept, but so necessary when one was out here on the edge of the frontier with only oneself and one's crew to rely on. It was an ability that had served him well as a starship captain.

It had taken several hours for the transporter operations to be complete and to get the *Enterprise* under way. And in those hours, Kirk was shocked to find that the condition of Hannah Faber had seriously deteriorated.

The captain received McCoy's report on the viewscreen in his own quarters where he'd gone to take a two-hour nap. He'd been running nonstop for over fifteen hours, but he felt he could afford only a short rest until they were under way.

"It's like the planetary DNA is unchecked and out of balance inside her. Her body is beginning to reject

the portions of her genome that are human," McCoy reported.

He recommended that she remain in sickbay indefinitely until the return, and Kirk readily agreed.

"Those bodyguards of hers aren't doing so well either. Ferlein's already in sickbay and out of commission. I'm keeping him sedated. That's about the best I can do. Hox is showing signs of collapse, but so far, he's hanging in there."

"Major Merling?"

"He seems to be holding up all right," McCoy answered. *"He's an immigrant, he's got the Vesbian DNA like they all do. It's just going to take a little longer to kill him."*

"Let's try to make sure none of them die," Kirk said. "Especially . . ."

McCoy softened his tone. *"I'll do my best, Jim."*

"I know you will, Bones."

"Rest," said McCoy. *"That's a medical order."*

"Will do. Kirk out." He turned off the viewscreen, lay back on his bed, and was soon out like a light, despite his worries. This was another ability Kirk had that had served him in good stead over the years: He was an expert at power napping.

Hannah Faber lay suffering and Kirk was reduced to visiting her in sickbay. Their time alone together was over.

The monitors of the *Enterprise*'s sickbay had never troubled Kirk before, but now they seemed oppressive to him, an assault on his senses when all he wanted to do was pay attention to Hannah. The monitors that hung above the beds seemed more harbingers of doom than medical instruments. He wished that Hannah could be anywhere else but here. Yet she required constant observation and instant support when her fading system needed boosting with an injection or infusion of yet another cocktail of chemicals designed to keep her alive just a little longer, until she could reestablish her quantum-entangled, seemingly mystical connection with her homeworld.

Hannah looked so drawn and sallow, and her voice was only a shadow of the strong, honeyed voice he remembered from only days before. And yet even in her collapsing state, Hannah was still very beautiful to Kirk. He found himself imagining what it would be like to spend years with her, to attend her through sicknesses, to know her as an old woman.

This thought was one that Kirk seldom allowed himself to think when it came to his other romances. As he was a Starfleet officer, any woman who signed on with him was signing on for a life of hardship and long absences. This was something he did not want to inflict on anyone who was not prepared for the consequences of loving a starship captain.

But here he was considering what a life with a woman who was absolutely and totally bound to her own planet would be like. Of one thing Kirk was certain: It would be very difficult. Seeing Hannah here in sickbay drove home to him that everything she had said about her condition and the condition of her world was correct: Vesbians would die if they had to be away from their planet for very long. He knew he was watching her die. However, Hannah had assured him that she was young and strong and that a seventeen-day voyage, while it might push the limits of Vesbian physiology, would not kill a healthy Vesbian. Kirk silently held her to that promise as he watched Hannah collapse into autoimmune chaos.

She remained conscious for the most part, and McCoy was able to alleviate the pain she must be feeling in some measure, but Hannah had insisted that nothing blur her mental processes. This meant that she spent long stretches awake, unable to sleep because of the slow burn of agony she felt within.

Kirk spent as much time as he could with her. They did not speak much, but he found that looking into Hannah's eyes was a kind of communication. At one point she whispered into his ear: "I think you are saving me, Jim. I underestimated how bad this would be. If you were not here, I believe that I would have succumbed to it. Thank you, my dear captain."

"You're welcome, Hannah," Kirk replied. He would have leaned down and kissed her, but he had found that any contact with her skin caused Hannah pain and bruising. So he contented himself with once again looking into her eyes with love, and hoping that she could perceive the depth of his feeling.

At times she was able to drift into a fitful sleep, and when McCoy was done with his duties, the doctor insisted he and Kirk share a drink, usually a shot of the Earth whiskey they both enjoyed.

McCoy, for his part, had not modified his reaction to the genetic manipulation on Vesbius. Kirk could see that Bones was not comfortable with his captain's attraction to someone who was no longer entirely human. Kirk tried to alleviate McCoy's concerns, but the doctor merely shrugged and said, "I'm sure that Lieutenant McGivers felt the same way when she fell in love with Khan."

"Are you suggesting that, whatever my feelings, I am somehow betraying humanity by being with her?" asked Kirk. "Doctor, do I need to remind you that I have always carried out my duty?" The ancient streets of New York flashed before him. Her fair face caught in the headlights . . . *Edith*. Kirk rubbed his forehead.

"What I'm asking you to do is step back for a moment. What I'm suggesting is that your own human nature may be betraying you," said McCoy.

"We are attracted as a species to perfect symmetry, perfect health, and perfect beauty. Hannah embodies those qualities. How much of Hannah's loveliness is the result of genetic tinkering? How much of it is appearance rather than reality? When evolution produces a beauty, you understand that an enormous amount of collective experience is necessarily encoded into the same genome as the beauty. You might even call it a sort of wisdom. Can you state that a genetically engineered human beauty is anything other than a mask over who knows *what* kind of thing inside?"

Kirk nodded toward where Hannah lay. "Well, she's not a beauty now, Bones, and I find my feelings have only deepened. The Vesbians denied that they have made any changes other than their correction for the autoimmune response within themselves."

"Let's say that I believe them," said McCoy. "We know what the consequences were."

Kirk knocked back his whiskey and slowly nodded. "I take your point, Doctor, but what's done is done and apparently cannot be undone—at least not in time to save the population of the colony. All we can do is *our* duty to help, don't you agree?"

"Does your duty include falling in love?"

Kirk looked up in surprise at the doctor. McCoy smiled and took a final sip of his own whiskey. "Just asking," he said.

"It might," said Kirk in reply. "Bones, it just might." He held out his glass for another round.

Hikaru Sulu entered his favorite recreational room, rec room six on deck three, with a feeling of relief. This was the rec area with a dedicated connection to the ship computer's library, and thus it offered a student as history-mad as Sulu plenty of material in which he might get lost in the glorious (if sometimes bloody) days of yore.

The last few days on the bridge had been some of the most difficult duty he'd ever pulled as helmsman. Keeping the *Enterprise* shooting through space at warp eight was not merely a matter of touching a few buttons and then letting her go. Maintaining course at such a speed, the upper end of what the *Enterprise* was capable of, required constant corrections at the controls. In conjunction with the ship computer, Sulu had had to fly her as he might a small craft. Hour after hour, he had not been able to let his attention wane even in the slightest, for it was quite possible that an uncorrected course error could rapidly escalate into a major crisis that might require precious hours to fix—hours that the people of Vesbius did not have to spare. He'd wanted to remain at the helm for another long shift today, but the captain had ordered him to take a breather.

Two days after the visit to Janus VI, he was still filled with thoughts of the strange underground warrens of the Horta. It had been a fascinating landing party, and Sulu wished to explore what was known about this incredible species. What he really wished he could do was to meet and speak to a Horta in the manner that Spock could. But, failing that, he at least wanted to be prepared when he would deal with them in person. The helmsman wanted to find out their likes and dislikes in order to do his duty, but also out of pure curiosity. He also wanted to find out if *any* other silicon-based species were in the data banks, even non-sentient ones, and how first contact with those species had been handled. The chance to encounter beings like the Horta was one of the reasons Sulu had signed on to Starfleet to begin with.

But when Sulu took his first step into the rec area toward the library, he heard a sniffing intake of breath and turned to see that Major Merling was sitting in a corner nearby having a drink.

"Oh, great, the Japanese are here!" he said in a contemptuous tone upon seeing Sulu enter. He shot the helmsman a look of displeasure, if not outright loathing.

What did I ever do *to that guy to deserve this?* Sulu thought. *Not only that, but I'm pretty sure that Merling has some Asian ancestry. It's clear from his appearance that he does.*

Sulu turned to Merling and asked, "Have I done something to offend you, Major?"

The Vesbian snorted in disbelief. "You would ask me that, wouldn't you? I suppose it means nothing to your sort."

"What are you talking about?"

"The murder of your betters, that's what I'm talking about," said Merling. "What you Japanese weaklings did to the Chinese over the centuries is despicable."

Sulu was not a confrontational sort, but he couldn't ignore this jibe. There were at least ten other people in the rec room at the moment, and they were listening in as well, wondering how Sulu would respond.

Try to be reasonable, Sulu thought. *Getting angry over what's long passed serves no purpose.*

Sulu walked across to Merling's table and sat down across from the major.

"You've got to be joking," said Sulu. "I'm from San Francisco. Anyway, that's ancient history. Japan? China? Earth is united, and we're in the Federation. We believe that people of all cultures must work together for the common good of the galaxy."

True, he *did* find Japanese history fascinating, and sometimes he even imagined himself a modern-day samurai. In any case, Sulu was just as interested in his own ancestors' more recent history, from their time spent in internment camps during a particularly benighted moment for a frightened United States during Earth's World War II to the rise of the Sulus as a prominent family in San Francisco.

He had a feeling Merling wouldn't take the slightest interest in such matters were Sulu to bring them up, The major seemed to be lost in his own particular delusions at the moment.

Merling pushed back from the table as if to distance himself from Sulu.

"The common good?" said Merling with a laugh. "Humanity gave up on its own common good centuries ago. We stopped trying to make ourselves better and settled for mediocrity. And that's what your Federation has gotten you: a galaxy of mediocrity. Well, you can have it."

"I don't accept your premise. The Federation strives to excel," said Sulu. "I am proud to serve as a Starfleet officer and believe that we are doing good work."

"That's what you've been taught to believe by your masters," Merling answered.

Sulu touched his own chin in puzzlement. "My . . . masters? And who might they be?"

"Those pointy-eared computers who never should've been allowed to join the Federation in the first place. Now *they* are the ones pulling the strings."

"Are you talking about Vulcans?" Sulu said.

"I am indeed," said Merling. "And speaking of genetic manipulation, take a look at the cold and calculated way they breed their stock. *They* know how to keep themselves in a dominant position over weaklings, humans and others."

"You're a Vulcan Domination conspiracy theorist?" Sulu said in amazement. He had heard about such people, but he'd never met one before.

"It's not a conspiracy when it's right out there in the open for anyone to see who has eyes," said Merling. "Only the cattle are too stupid to recognize that they're being fattened up for a purpose."

What a quack. But then Sulu considered an alternate explanation: Maybe this was some sort of adverse reaction to medication.

"Have you been taking your autoimmune vaccine?" Sulu asked.

"I have, and what the devil does that have to do with anything?"

"And you've experienced no . . . adverse reactions? Chief Advisor Faber has become quite ill, I believe."

Merling nodded knowingly and chuckled. "The children of Vesbius. Greatness built into their genes—*engineered*—and yet they refuse to take the next step."

"What would that be?"

"To throw off the Vulcan yoke," spat out Merling. "To take humanity's rightful place in the galaxy."

"Major Merling," Sulu said respectfully, "I think I'll get to my library studies now."

Sulu stood up and made to leave the table.

As quickly as the look of rage had passed over Merling's face, he seemed to gain control and stifle it. "Please excuse me, Ensign—"

"Lieutenant."

"Lieutenant, I mean," Merling said. "Yes, I have to admit that I'm not feeling myself. The injections are perhaps starting to take their toll."

"Can I help in any way?"

The snarling Merling returned as quickly as it had fled.

"I don't want your aid, *hinomoto oniko*," said Merling in a low voice. The ancient insult meant "son of a devil"—a Chinese slur against Japanese soldiers.

Sulu thought it more amusing than insulting. He shrugged. "You know, if all that you say is true, what could we 'cattle' do about it? It seems that you believe we are not even capable of becoming aware of our own situation."

"I would say you ought to rise up against the bastards," Merling said. "But it's too late for that. That man Khan, he had the right idea. You met him, didn't you?"

"I had that misfortune," Sulu replied evenly. He put his hands on the back of the chair he stood behind.

Guess I'll stay a little longer and jawbone with this maniac, he thought. *It's still possible I may be able to talk some reason into him after all.*

Merling had brought up one of Sulu's most distasteful memories.

He had felt an instant dislike for the product of the Earth Eugenics Wars that had been brought aboard the *Enterprise.* His aversion had begun even before Khan showed his true colors and attempted to take over the *Enterprise,* almost killing the captain in a decompression chamber before he could be stopped. Sulu's admiration for Kirk had been stoked higher when the captain had sentenced the Augment to life on a harsh unsettled planet instead of handing him over to Starfleet. It had been a bold move, one that Sulu had not thought of and that had only increased his desire to learn by serving with such an extraordinary captain.

"If Khan had won his war all those centuries ago," said Merling, "humanity might have been able to stand up to the Vulcans and not become their chattel." Merling shook his head and took another drink from his glass. Sulu saw now that Merling was pretty far in his cups, and what he was listening to was more drunk rambling than coherent philosophy.

"Well, I must do a little research on a library computer," said Sulu. "So if you'll excuse me, Major."

Merling abruptly stood up. He glared at Sulu.

"Go about your business, *hinomoto oniko,* and I'll go about mine."

For moment, Sulu believed that Merling might physically leap across the table and attack him. He was quite certain that he could take the major out with a couple of blows, but then he would have so much explaining to do and so much paperwork that it was not worth the satisfaction he would get from putting the major in his place.

But Merling had solved the problem for Sulu by breaking off his gaze and then stumbling out of the rec room. Sulu, still standing with his hands on the chair in front of the table where Merling had been, looked after the exiting major in befuddlement.

"Well, you sure are cool under fire, Lieutenant," said one of the ensigns in the rec room. "I'd have been tempted to brain that moron."

Sulu smiled. "Not enough brains there to knock out," he replied. "And definitely not worth the effort to find them."

There was muted laughter around the rec room, and Sulu made his way to his intended destination.

What a strange, unhappy man, he thought. *I have a very bad feeling about him. Not unlike the feeling I had when I first saw the* Botany Bay.

Sulu decided his Horta research could wait. He wasn't sure what Merling might be up to—probably just slinking back to his cabin. But whatever it was, he was going to find out. And for that, a bit of research on Major Merling might be in order.

Major Merling stumbled down the corridor a few steps. When he got out of the line of sight of the rec room entrance, he straightened up and began walking in a sober manner.

So easy to fool the cattle, Merling thought to himself. *Enjoyable as well.*

It had been necessary that he appear drunk in order to establish an alibi for what he was going to do next. While Merling had once believed he had a ally in Kirk and the *Enterprise*—however misguided the Starfleet captain and his benighted crew actually were—it had soon become apparent that, while they were all for getting the Vesbians to evacuate the planet surface and find a new home, the reasons they wished to do this were counterproductive, to Merling and the Exos movement.

Merling was keenly aware that he was *not* an original settler. He had come to Vesbius after serving as a mercenary in several planetary forces inside and outside the Federation. What had been a job as a hired military chief to the chancellor had become a calling after the planet had begun to destroy his immune system. At that time, he'd had to make the choice to either stay and receive the genetic alteration necessary to avoid the autoimmune rejection by the Vesbius biosphere, or move on.

Merling hated to remember that part of his life. The problem was that Vesbius was the last stop on the descending path of a military career that had not been distinguished to begin with. Merling had no offers anywhere else, and he had nowhere to go. He supposed he could have taken some sort of security billet on a merchant ship and gotten the hell off the planet in time to save himself from having to undergo the change, but he delayed until it was too late, and it was either receive the genetic alteration or die in a hospital bed on Vesbius. At that time, Merling had made a virtue of necessity and loudly proclaimed that he was ready to become a real Vesbian.

Like many converts to necessity, once he was fully a member of the society, Merling forgot his previous objections to the population—he'd once called Vesbians freaks of nature—and instead began to glory in his new condition. He sought out those who felt the same way he did, those who believed that the change had not only made Vesbians different, but *superior* to humans: the Exos movement.

Finally, he'd found a place to fit in. Be someone important. Be recognized as the superior man he felt himself to be.

An Exo understood this essential truth, and then it came time to *act* on it. To make changes. Exos, forced underground by edict of the Vesbian

Council, had been engaged in going further than the mere adaptation alteration. Why not use the opportunity of the crisis on the planet to get rid of the old settler deadwood attitudes and ring in a new future?

What mattered wasn't Vesbius the planet but the superior product that planet had produced.

Vesbians.

Merling began to see himself as the vanguard for a change in galactic history. He'd worried about his own courage and heroism before, particularly under fire. He'd had several bad experiences on his previous assignments in that regard, experiences he tried hard to forget. But now Merling worried about his place in the grand scheme of things no longer. And when the asteroid had been discovered, he knew that this was another moment of chaos and crisis and it was his duty to exploit it. He had to use this opportunity to press the Vesbians beyond their mere alterations and onward toward becoming something better than what they had been before. The pressure of the autoimmune rejection illness that a general evacuation would precipitate would drive the Vesbians to engage in quick and massive genetic tinkering to save themselves and their children. They would make themselves better in the process, better able to withstand the rigors of planetary settlement than they ever had been before, better than humans ever had been.

They would finish what the ancient Augments

were never allowed to finish. They would make themselves into the natural successors of *Homo sapiens*, Merling believed. With the subtle manipulation of humanity from within, and with Merling's foresight directing the movement, Vesbians would emerge as the natural rulers of the galaxy—and especially of humanity. Humans were their ancestors; therefore they would be their natural subjects. It was going to happen sooner or later, Merling believed. He wanted to be the one to bring it about and the one to reap its initial benefits. Perhaps one day there would be a statue of him on Earth: the man—no *super* man—who was the father of a new, better human race.

The major made his way carefully back to his quarters, trying to pass through as many of the crowded corridors of the ship as he could. He made sure to bump into a few crew members along the way and give them reason to remember him with either an apology or a harsh word. It didn't matter which, so long as he left an impression. Finally, he arrived at his quarters in junior officer country and slipped inside. It was all part of his job.

If any creatures in the galaxy did not deserve his Vesbian respect, it was those bugs from Janus VI. Not only was it his duty to further precipitate the crisis on Vesbius until the desired outcome could be accomplished, but he also considered it a sacred duty to eradicate this infestation of roaches that the Vulcan had talked the weak captain into shipping straight to a human world.

Merling brought out a communicator that he had concealed and brought aboard the ship. It was tuned to a little-used subspace frequency and double-scrambled for maximum secrecy. There was a matching communicator elsewhere on board.

"Head One. Head One calling Hand."

After a momentary pause, an answer came over the communicator: "*Hand here. I do not have much time. I am on a short break.*"

"The time has come to put a stop to the pollution," Merling said.

"*As you say, Head. When she was touring the shuttle bay and touching those creatures, I released your powder. I have the activation device ready.*"

"Excellent."

"*Head . . .*" There was a momentary pause on the other end.

"Yes, what is it?" Still no reply. "Hand? Hand, answer me."

A crackling response finally arrived over the communicator: "*Phase two of the plan . . . I do not believe . . . I can't do it, sir.*"

Merling sighed. Weakness. Why must he always be surrounded by weakness? He put the communicator back to his lips and spoke in a low, clear voice.

"You realize that I have the entire planetary vaccine supply in my control."

"Yes, I . . . I suppose you do."

"And here on the ship, do you think it was an accident that the chief advisor was experiencing autoimmune rejection syndrome so early? And what about Ferlein?"

"No, I . . . I supposed I preferred not to think about it, sir."

"Well think about it now. They have received only half-strength vaccines. The fool ship's surgeon trusted the supply I provided and has administered incorrect dosages. If you fail at carrying out your instructions, I will do to you what I have done to the chief advisor. Do you understand?"

A very long pause this time. Finally, a reply: "I . . . do."

"Good," said Merling. "I know you are committed. You will not allow it to come to that because you will do what is right."

Merling closed his communicator and lay back on his bed, not bothering to take off his boots. It would be even better if he fell asleep—any life-sign readings in the compartment would show him snoozing—but he was too excited for that. He wished he did not have to resort to subterfuge but could confront his enemy head-on.

The warrior who wins is the one who lives to fight another day, Merling told himself.

The fight must go on. Against the Vulcan conspiracy. Against utterly alien devils such as the Horta who sought to taint the very breathing space of humanity.

Worst of all, they meant to entangle Vesbius in their depravity and decadence.

Vulcan manipulation, the desire to contaminate the pure stock of Vesbius with outside ideas and, eventually, outside blood. Outside DNA. To destroy what was better. Merling was not surprised at such perfidy in lesser species, although, as always, he could not contain his disgust no matter how many times he encountered it. Horta, Vulcan, Klingon . . . even humans. The galaxy would be a better place without any of them, and Merling was happy to do his part to bring that about.

The time of purification would come sooner rather than later—but come it would. He knew that, no matter what happened, he was on the right side of history. But, unlike Khan, he would see his revolution through.

Ten

The alarm went off on the bridge just as Kirk was attempting to take a sip of his coffee. Wasn't that always the way? He quickly handed it back to the yeoman who had brought it to him.

Kirk pressed the intership button on his chair. "What do you have, Scotty?"

"Captain, I was picking up a power drain from some unknown source, and then I noticed that there was a pressure change associated with it. I ran a scan, and, believe it or not, we have a breach. I'm attempting to pinpoint it."

A hull breach. The worst disaster in space. It was almost unheard of in Starfleet. Ships were not only made of extremely tough stuff necessary for interstellar travel, but the exterior was reinforced with force fields to contain atmosphere and to keep out the radiation that a breach might produce.

"Where, Scotty? Have you found it?" Kirk asked. He felt the adrenaline rising within him.

"Captain, you're not gonna like this, but the breach is in the shuttle bay," Mister Scott reported.

"Do you think one of the Horta has somehow disregarded our warnings and burned a hole in a bulkhead?"

"I don't think so," Kirk answered. "How bad is it?"

"From the power drain, I'd say it's fairly large," Scotty said. *"I'll get a team on it right now. It looks like the shuttle bay doors failed."*

"That's impossible. That thing has a dozen failsafes," Kirk said. He shook his head. This smelled very fishy, and he wanted to investigate himself. "I'll head for the shuttle bay. Have an EV suit standing by."

"Aye, sir," Scotty said.

"Full stop, Mister Sulu! Take us out of warp and maintain our position."

"Yes, sir."

"You have the bridge, Sulu." Kirk rose from his chair.

Chekov was manning the science station. "Ensign, get every sensor we have on the area we just passed through. Backtrack as far as you can."

"Yes, Captain."

Kirk strode quickly to the turbolift, almost running into Spock. "Come with me, Spock," said Kirk. "We have a situation in the shuttle bay."

When Kirk arrived, he saw that the interior airlock was fully engaged, cutting off the crew from the main shuttle bay area. It was only possible to open the airlock without expelling atmosphere if the shuttle bay shields were working, but that was not the case. The doors were partway open—this much could be seen through the airlock port—and the atmospheric gauge beside the airlock read near zero for the interior. Kirk turned and asked Spock, "What do we know about the Horta and a vacuum? Can they withstand it?"

Spock reached over and touched the door. A troubled expression crossed his face for a moment, but then he returned to his usual placid indifference. "I am too far away for anything but the most tentative of communication. I am detecting signs of distress within, however, but not due to suffocation or other physical deterioration. What I feel is dismay and fright."

"Captain, this is the bridge," said Chekov's voice over intership. *"Sensors indicate that several Horta have been ejected from the shuttle bay and have fallen out of hyperspace into Newtonian space-time."*

"Life signs, Mister Chekov."

After a moment's delay, Chekov reported back: *"Sir, I am detecting fifteen independent readings."*

"They're alive?"

"For the time being," Chekov answered.

"Can you get a lock to beam them aboard?"

"Not yet, sir. They are too far, three groups clumped together, but each scattered over ten thousand four hundred kilometers."

"Captain, this is Sulu. I have brought the ship about. We should be in range within minutes."

"Let's hope they have minutes," Kirk said. "All right. Good work, bridge. Report any changes to me."

"Can we get the force field up?"

"The shuttle bay force field is intended only to maintain atmospheric pressure for the time it takes for a shuttle to pass through. If we are unable to close the shuttle bay doors, pressurizing the bay will be ineffective. The force field will fail and the air will be expelled."

"Then we have to get the doors closed, and fast," Kirk said.

"Affirmative, Captain," said Spock.

The repair team was now suited up, and Kirk began to step into the suit they had brought for him.

"If I may, sir," said Spock.

Kirk cut him off. "Spock? "

"Captain, it makes more sense for *me* to accompany the rescue crew," Spock said. "I have a rapport with the Horta, and their aid may be essential in resolving the situation."

Kirk considered. There was something telling him viscerally to do something.

Spock was right. "Agreed." He thrust the EV suit at Spock. "Get going."

The repair team opened the airlock door, stepped inside, and closed it behind them. Then there was a *whoosh* as the exterior door opened and the small atmosphere inside the airlock rushed into the vacuum of the shuttle bay. They sensibly held on to avoid being pulled forward by the negative air pressure.

The crew rushed into the shuttle bay toward the crescent-shaped opening on the right side of the hatch. As Spock approached it, he observed that the doors were not fully open. One of the flanged components of the iris door had been retracted, leaving a space that was 3.02 meters wide. The width was just enough for a Horta to be sucked through.

As Spock and the crew drew nearer to the huge bay doors, the emergency lights, still functioning overhead even in the hard vacuum, revealed that the way forward was blocked. Huddled Horta surrounded the shuttle bay door. Judging from the arrangement, it seemed the Horta had been pulled toward the open door by the huge rush of atmospheric discharge and were now clumped together at the opening.

The problem now was to get the shuttle bay door closed. But first Spock must assess the state of the remaining Horta. They were not moving. When Spock reached the first of them, he saw the reason for this.

The Horta had not merely held on, they had dissolved part of the deck in order to weld themselves inside the shuttle bay. Each of the creatures was sunken in a Horta-shaped declivity of nearly a half-meter depth, and they looked as if they were resting in their own giant footprints. They had made their own safety holds, in effect, in order to not be pulled out into space.

Clever, Spock thought. *Also extremely logical.*

Spock allowed himself to dip once more into the Horta collective consciousness.

Alarm, alarm! The sucking, pulling winds! The flow outward into the void! Falling, falling! We must stick tight.

Stick tight. Fuse. Hold to the not-rock under our carapace!

Spock made his presence known to the Horta with a quick signal of thought—Spock pictured this signal as a blue flame within his mind—and then spoke directly to the Horta hive mind.

We will discover the cause of what has happened and attempt to resolve the problem, Spock thought to them.

Speaker from the Stars, All Mother to Be, you have come to save us!

I am not the All Mother, and I may never be, Spock thought back to them. *But I will do my best to help. It is necessary that I make my way by climbing over you.*

All is forgiven, Speaker from the Stars. He is the savior. The bringer of truth! The All Mother is here to protect us!

I am not *your mother,* Spock thought one final

time, but he could feel that it was a useless pronouncement at the moment. These Horta were frightened, and the only safety they had previously known was the All Mother's benign presence.

Spock keyed on the microphone in his EV suit helmet. "Repair team, this is Spock. I'm afraid were going to have to do something that may disconcert our alien guests. I can see no other way to the shuttle bay control room than to walk over the backs of the Horta."

"Walk on their backs, sir?" said one of the rescue squad members. *"Won't we dissolve into them, like if we stepped into lava or something?"*

"Negative," said Spock. "The dangerous portion of the creature is on the bottom, Ensign." Spock considered that, in this instance, showing might be better than telling. He leaped up onto the back of the nearest Horta and perched there, as if he were on the shell of an enormous turtle. "Follow me, Officers."

He stepped from Horta to Horta as if they were stones in a brook crossing and made his way across the shuttle bay until he reached his intended destination: shuttle bay auxiliary control, where the manual override was located.

Auxiliary control was normally a pressurized cabin in which an operator could open and close the enormous shuttle bay doors safely in atmospheric confinement. The door to the control panel booth was jammed, and the rescue crew immediately set about torching it open with phasers to get inside. Spock peered through the window to the control panel within.

The shuttle bay manual override, which was set in a panel within the control room, was only for emergency use, and when it was engaged the assumption was that the atmosphere in the shuttle bay had already been cleared out, or that whoever was in the shuttle bay was prepared for the evacuation of the air. Nobody in his right mind would engage the mechanism without adequate warning and a direct order. In fact, it was locked against accidental triggering by a see-through covering. Spock saw that this covering shield had disintegrated entirely, as if it had been neatly cut from its support structure by a knife that could cut through pure crystal.

Spock's Academy-trained mind immediately recognized this for what it was.

Military nanotechnology.

Spock spoke rapidly into his EV suit communicator. "Repair and rescue crew, this is Spock. Immediately back away from the shuttle bay doors control room and form a line to prevent any Horta from venturing in this direction. Repeat, immediately retreat and form a cordon at least three meters from the doorway. Military-grade nanotechnology is suspected."

Spock looked outside and saw the repair crew

stopped in their tracks. Nano was frightening stuff. And the use of military nano was a war crime within the Federation. "Quickly," Spock told them.

Spock's orders seemed to wake them and the engineers did as instructed. Spock entered the cubicle and examined the control panel. It was not visibly damaged.

He reached down and brushed the surface. The metal—at least it *had* been metal—crumbled beneath the brush of his gloved hand to reveal the electronic innards of the controls.

Fused. Destroyed.

And yet the damage seemed self-contained. Someone who knew how to use nanotechnology had done this.

"Interesting," Spock said. Trailing out from the fused mass of wires and circuitry was a tiny silver strand, a filament no more than a hair's breadth thick. It hung down across the manual override panel like a long, wispy hair from a horse's mane.

Spock keyed his suit transceiver to engage with the ship's communication system and called up Scott. "Engineering, this is Spock. I have discovered a nanotechnological deployment in the auxiliary shuttle bay door control. It appears to be low-grade nanotech that requires activation from an outside source—"

"*Aye*," said Mister Scott, after presumably taking a moment to digest what Spock was reporting.

The first officer was impressed by how quickly Scott grasped complex situations involving technology and machinery. *"So have you found an antenna?"*

"Astute, Mister Scott," replied Spock. "I have indeed. It is monofilament—" Spock looked at his tricorder readings. "And appears to be pure pergium."

"Mister Spock, you're not saying . . . could the Horta have done this? That is the main mineral they're mining on Janus VI, after all."

"Negative, Mister Scott," Spock replied. "Pergium is used extensively in both transporter and subspace communication equipment."

"It's a subspace receiver."

"That is my tentative conclusion. A part of the triggering mechanism."

"Can we . . . untrigger it? Have the nano rebuild the control panel?"

Spock again checked his tricorder readout on the material.

"Negative. The nano has deactivated and scrambled its previous programming. Someone was attempting to cover his tracks, Mister Scott. However, for this size subspace antenna to function would require a subspace receiver keyed to very high frequencies and within relatively close range, judging by the diameter of the antenna. The transmitter must be located on the ship, yet use frequencies very different from those commonly used aboard."

"You're talking sabotage from within, Mister Spock," said Mister Scott.

"Indeed."

Spock continued, "Mister Scott, I am going to destroy this antenna. I would like for you to monitor and observe whether this elicits a subspace callback. If it does, you should be able to pinpoint the source."

"Aye, sir," Scotty said. *"That I can do. Standing by."*

Spock realized his phaser was too powerful for what he intended to do. He looked around for another tool and his eyes lit upon a glassed-in cabinet that contained a titanium hammer. This was not standard issue for the control room but another one of Mister Scott's personal design upgrades to the *Enterprise,* one Spock was very glad of at the moment. The glass case had a label: "For Emergency Use Only. Break Glass." Spock used his elbow to shatter the glass, then retrieved the hammer. With a deft stroke, he brought it down in the middle of the little monofilament wire. Like all pergium, its tensile strength was virtually nonexistent, and it shattered into fragments as if it were of crystalline structure.

"Antenna destroyed. Anything, Mister Scott?" Spock asked.

"Sir, I got the smallest flash of the return signal," said Scott. *"Almost as if someone thought the thing had failed and was trying to turn it back on, then*

realized their mistake and shut down quickly. I don't know what to make of it."

"Did you locate the source?"

"Deck five, corridor two, compartments A through G, sir."

"That is sickbay, Mister Scott."

"Aye, sir. It is. Now who do you suppose would have the control for that thing in sickbay?"

Spock remained silent. Once again, without the facts, speculation was illogical. But it did not escape his attention that the one anomalous patient in sickbay at the moment was none other than Hannah Faber.

"The signal could be some kind of delayed mechanism, a plant," Mister Scott said. *"I know the Vesbians have mixed feelings about the Horta, but surely she would never stoop to* this."

Spock overrode the control panel by creating a relay through the manual hatch closing toggle. The bay doors began to slide shut, soundless in the vacuum, and then—

Stopped.

Spock cycled the power again, flipped the manual toggle.

Nothing, no sound. But a nearby gauge showed a power surge building. The doors were trying to shut, but something was jammed. He knew that if there had been air in the shuttle bay, he would hear the door closing mechanisms grinding away.

"Mister Scott, we have another problem."

"*What's that, Mister Spock?*"

"The iris panels have closed unevenly, and the guide plate is disengaged," said Spock. "I cannot close the door using the manual override." He looked out the window and examined the base of the door. It was worse than he had thought. "Furthermore, the glide track itself is mangled. The shuttle bay doors will not close. The Horta may be vacuum resistant, but they are not immune to its effects."

Even now, Spock could hear the calls of the Horta hive mind.

It hurts. The bubbles within hurt and harm. Help us, Speaker from the Stars! Help us, All Mother to Be! We are your children, and we are in pain!

"Sickbay?" Kirk was taken aback. He had been standing outside the shuttle bay main entrance listening to the communicator traffic and wishing he was inside. This was one of the hardest parts of being captain: delegation.

"Scotty," Kirk asked, cutting in, "can the reading be due to equipment malfunction?"

"*No, sir,*" said Mister Scott. "*It came from sickbay.*"

"What the devil's going on?" Kirk wondered aloud. "All right, Scotty, get down here and help Spock. I'll be expecting one of your miracles."

"Aye, sir," Scott replied.

"Kirk to bridge. Mister Sulu, interior sensor sweep. Have Chekov locate all Vesbians onboard."

"Scanning," reported Chekov. *"Major Merling in his quarters. The other three are in sickbay."*

"That's all. Kirk out."

It has to be the bodyguard who isn't experiencing the autoimmune response. What was his name?

Hox.

Hannah was in danger.

"Bridge, seal off sickbay. Notify McCoy. Have a security team meet me there on the double."

"Aye, sir."

Kirk raced off down the corridor toward the lift and sickbay, ten decks away.

In sickbay, Doctor McCoy prepared another I.V. for Hannah Faber. Hox, one of the so-called aides, had returned from a short break and taken up his usual vulturelike position a few feet away from Hannah. McCoy did not at all approve of having the man in his sickbay. The other, Ferlein, was in a coma, hovering near death.

McCoy wasn't sure what electrolyte balance would best preserve the Vesbian woman or her aide, but he had few options at this point. There was no cure for a body that was actively rejecting its own organs. Immunosuppressant might help a *human* avoid autoimmune reaction, but this had actually *accelerated* the breakdown in the Vesbian system. McCoy as yet had no idea why this was the case. Whatever those Vesbian scientists had done, they had certainly made it impossible for them to be treated by conventional means when they *did* get sick, McCoy thought.

While McCoy was checking the readings, he heard someone quietly step up behind him and felt a blow on the back of his neck.

The world went white with pain, and then black as McCoy collapsed to the floor.

The doctor groggily got to his feet to witness a most horrifying sight. The bodyguard Hox, it seemed, was attempting to suffocate Hannah Faber with a sickbay pillow.

McCoy made a grab for Hox's arm. "What the hell are you doing?" McCoy yelled into the man's ear.

"Let me go!" shouted Hox. "You fool, he'll kill my family!"

Hox shook his body mightily, but this failed to dislodge McCoy. He then let go of the pillow long enough to savagely push McCoy back. McCoy stumbled across sickbay and into a rack of medical instruments. He fell on top of skittering stainless steel and duroceramic clamps, blades, and scissors—

And what was that? That lump against his back? McCoy flipped over and reached for the lump.

It was a laser scalpel, a small cylinder that fit neatly into McCoy's palm.

As he rose, McCoy saw Hox standing by Hannah's bedside and attempting, once again, to stuff the pillow over her face and suffocate her. She was faintly struggling, but in her weakened state, Hox was likely to succeed.

Stalking up behind Hox as quietly as he could, McCoy put an arm around the Vesbian's neck. With his other hand, McCoy pressed the scalpel into the middle of Hox's back.

Hox snarled, but before he could make another move, McCoy gripped him tightly by the shoulder and spoke slowly and carefully into the bodyguard's ear.

"This is a laser scalpel, Mister Hox," McCoy said. "It can be adjusted from fifteen millimeters to twenty centimeters in length. If I set it for a short length, I cut your spinal cord in half. If I set it for long, the blade will reach into the chambers of your heart."

McCoy felt Hox shudder in his grip, but his pressure on the pillow remained firm. He increased his choke hold on the Vesbian's neck and leaned very close to one ear.

"Since you won't release that pillow, I have to ask you: What's it going to be, Hox? Your heart or your spinal column? I haven't got all day, and I have other patients to tend to."

McCoy gave a poke with the scalpel handle, and Hox gasped. With a cry of frustration, the Vesbian let go of his hold on the pillow. McCoy backed up, dragging him from the sickbay bed, never letting go.

He heard Hannah gasping, unable to regain her breath.

Have to get to her soon, McCoy thought. *But now I've got this Vesbian on my hands.*

And then Kirk and two red-shirted security officers burst through the door. They headed straight for Hox and McCoy.

Hox twisted in McCoy's grip with great strength—perhaps *superhuman* strength, McCoy thought—and snatched the laser scalpel away from the doctor.

With the laser scalpel in his hand, Hox lunged at the captain.

Kirk ducked under the lunge and punched Hox in the gut. The Vesbian stumbled back, catching his breath. But now murder was in his eyes.

"I'll cut you, normal," Hox said. He held the laser scalpel before him and pressed the extension button.

A red light flashed, but nothing happened.

"What is this?" screamed Hox. He turned to McCoy. "How do you work this, normal scum?"

This was all the opening Kirk needed. He moved in with a roundhouse punch that sent Hox reeling.

The laser scalpel flew from his hand. Hox growled in frustration.

"If I fail, they're all going to die!" he shouted, and he charged the two security officers who guarded the door. They were taken by surprise and immediately drew their phasers.

"No!" Kirk shouted, but it was too late.

Energy whine and flash of power.

Hox collapsed on the floor.

"Phaser setting?" Kirk demanded of the security officers.

"Full stun, sir," one of the security officers answered. "Standard emergency protocol. He'll be out for hours."

"Yes," said Kirk ruefully. "Fine, but it will also be hours before we can question him. Good work, though. Take him to the brig."

As the security team moved to do their captain's bidding, Kirk rushed over to Hannah.

She was gasping for breath but still alive. He held her hand. "Hannah . . ." he said in a plaintive tone.

Without another word, McCoy rushed over to Hannah's sickbed with a hypo. "Tri-ox."

Hannah was breathing on her own. McCoy glanced at the life systems readout above the bed, then stood back beside Kirk and put a hand on his shoulder.

"She'll live, Jim," he said.

After a moment Hannah roused to a semiconscious state. "My *own* man. How can it be? How can they have gotten to him? He was . . . he was trying to . . ."

"Best to be quiet now," McCoy said. "Conserve your energy. You're safe." He nodded toward Kirk. "The captain is here."

"My captain," Hannah whispered with relief.

"Hannah."

It was only after he was sure that Hannah was out of immediate danger that Kirk found McCoy in his office. This time it was McCoy, and not Kirk, who needed a drink. He was still shivering from the confrontation with Hox.

Kirk poured out a round and each man sipped a shot.

"So you held a laser scalpel to a man and threatened to shank him?" said Kirk. "Why Bones, I didn't know you had such a cold-blooded killer instinct in you."

"I don't," McCoy said. He held up the scalpel and showed it to Kirk. A flashing red indicator light blinked weakly. "The scalpel's power supply was depleted and I knew it all along. I had it on the stand recharging." McCoy shook his head in wonder at his own audacity. "I may as well have stuck a salt shaker in his back."

"I'm going to get to the bottom of this," Kirk said. "Hannah doesn't believe he was acting alone, and neither do I. But we have more pressing matters to worry about at the moment."

"What's that?" asked McCoy.

"Physical forces, Bones," said Kirk. "Space—and time. How long those Horta can withstand the vacuum, to be precise."

Captain's log. Stardate 6414.3. The Enterprise has been sabotaged. The shuttle bay has been breached by nanotechnological means, and an attempt has been made on the Vesbian ambassador and chief advisor, Hannah Faber. We have captured the would-be assassin. I've ordered the remaining Vesbian aboard, Major Johan Merling, confined to quarters, but there is no evidence against him as yet, and the nanotechnological sabotage may have been planted when the Vesbians came aboard for treatment. My main priority is rescuing the Horta who were pulled into space and securing the shuttle bay from vacuum damage.

When Captain Kirk returned to the shuttle bay airlock entrance, he found his first officer and chief engineer in an intense discussion over what step to take next. They were going over the technical details of the operation of the shuttle bay doors, and how they might be effectively shut, now that the main operating mechanism had been destroyed by the nanotech weapon.

Scotty was outside the airlock door, while Spock was on the other side, still in his EV suit. The two were speaking through the transparent aluminum window via Spock's suit communicator. It appeared that they had just arrived at an agreement on a plan of action.

"Aye, it could work," said Scotty.

"Gentlemen," said Kirk, "I trust you have a plan?"

Scott turned to the captain and shook his head. "More a wild notion than a plan, sir. I can't get the doors closed by any means before we make repairs," he said. "But Mister Spock says that the Horta are feeling very uncomfortable. We're going to have to either evacuate them or figure out a way to seal off the shuttle bay."

"*The Horta have a suggestion, Captain, and I believe it is a good one,*" said Spock. "*They are capable of very fine precision when using the rock dissolving secretions on their undercarriages. They say if we can supply them with the appropriate materials to form a chemical weld, they will be able to seal the doors sufficiently to repressurize the shuttle bay environment until repairs can be effected on the door mechanism.*"

Kirk turned to Scott. "What kind of material do they need, Scotty? Is this even possible?"

"Aye," said Scotty, scratching his head. "We can turn a number of the empty storage barrels in the main cargo bay into the proper material. They're made of a mettalic alloy that should be strong enough when heated. Of course, that will leave us without any transport storage containers until we can get some more. If we had to make a rescue run carrying grain or some other material that required bulk storage, we'd be out of luck, Captain."

"Understood," said Kirk, "but let's give the Horta the chance to make this repair. Do you have a way to get the barrels to them?"

"The cargo bay is one deck below us," said Scotty. "I figure I seal off a bulkhead down there, depressurize. Maybe then Mister Spock could ask some of his wee creatures to cut a hole through the deck, and we can pass the barrels up using antigravity lifts."

"*They're not my 'wee creatures,'*" said Mister Spock, "*but fully autonomous beings in their own right. Nevertheless, I believe the Horta will agree readily enough. I think the effort to contain their secretions and not burn a hole through the deck has been a source of minor difficulty to them on the trip so far, and they will relish the chance to . . . dissolve something.*"

"All right," said Kirk. "Let's get on it. Meanwhile, I'm going to the bridge. Mister Spock, tell the Horta that we're going to find every last one of their missing kin. And then I'm going to bring the monster who perpetrated this act to justice."

An hour later, the welding job began. The Horta did not waste time disassembling the barrels but gently dissolved portions of their surface, welded them together, and chemically annealed them in a process that Scott reported was fascinating and innovative. It all seemed a bit jury-rigged to Kirk, but Scotty seemed pleased as the crescent-shaped amalgamation of storage barrels began to take shape like a giant clump of frog's eggs in a creek.

The Horta assembled the containment barrier by climbing on the sides of the shuttle bay hatch itself, starting from the top and working down. It was very much like watching bees build a hive. The reconstruction was done in small parts, and very quickly. The welds themselves were chemical and not ultra-high temperature, so only smoke and no sparks arose from them. In the vacuum of the large shuttle bay, the smoke quickly dissipated, and since there was no draft, it spread out in uniform fashion from the weld point. Nevertheless, the entire process had an industrial feel to it, as if a huge Horta factory was at work, and it was fascinating to watch.

Finally, the last weld was put in place, and the Horta reported that they were finished. After checking the readings, Scott repressurized the shuttle bay. There was the rushing of air as the shuttle bay was oxygenated. Spock heard what he believed was a collective sigh from the Horta outside, but it was more like a rumble of thunder. The Horta could survive in a vacuum, but their time limit for exposure had approached maximum. All readings soon returned to nominal, and Spock took off his EV helmet. The other members of the repair team did likewise, and at last the airlock door opened.

The Horta aboard the *Enterprise* were safe.

As to those who had been sucked out—their fate remained to be determined.

Eleven

The Horta known as Slider Dan to the humans was fascinated by what was happening to him and around him. There had been the moment of decompression, followed by the enormous tug of the atmosphere pulling his massive body toward the open doors. Before he could dig in or establish a chemical hold—he was floating in space.

It was like surfacing on Janus VI—but so much *more*. More everything. More sky. More space. No gravitational tug. There were several others with him who had almost instantaneously been pulled out just as he was. The tumble from subspace into normal space was a rush like none he'd experienced.

First of all, there was the physical sensation: the tumble and roll of being in a place where no gravity, either natural or artificial, existed. A Horta always knew the way up and down, but these directions ceased to apply with the suddenness and profound completeness that shocked the system like nothing had done before.

And then crossing the bubble of subspace into

normal space had shaken his mind as forcefully as falling out had shaken his body. There was a moment where both bubble universe and larger universe coexisted, where the stars were both near and far away at the same moment, and there was a double perception of everything. This was not merely a change in infrared perception but a change in awareness. It was like being in two places at once, like carving through rock and being at rest at the same time.

There was the shudder in the digestive cavity and the feeling of reality caving in all around him and then reestablishing itself, like one of his bad dreams of a tunnel collapse. When he'd first had those dreams, he'd gone to the All Mother and told her about them. She had explained that they were not that unusual among his kind and that a dream could teach you something, even if it wasn't something that you could use directly. Dreams were ways of exploring feelings, and feelings must be mastered by a young Horta. Feelings were what had nearly destroyed the clans in the past, and while feelings were necessary, immature Horta needed to know how to keep them in check and use them in moments of need, and to not be overcome by them.

Then came the overwhelming sense of complete aloneness. So much of a Horta's existence was spent pressed up against walls or against other Horta, and being shaped by those contacts. Slider Dan for the first time felt nothing pressing in or pulling him from any side. His mind was also free of the hive, completely free, for the first time.

He knew himself in that moment. He was a very small thing in the universe, but something that was alive and full of thoughts and perceptions, and, Slider Dan realized, in that moment, he was somebody.

Somebody who wanted to stay alive.

Slider Dan sent out his thoughts to discover if there was any possibility of connection with his kin. To his immense surprise and relief . . . someone answered.

Around Slider Dan were the thoughts of four others who had been sucked out with him. He could not see them in the darkness, for there was no light to reflect off of them except the light from stars hundreds of millions of kilometers away. But he could feel the minds of the others, their presence within telepathy range. He realized that this told him something.

They must be fairly close by. For the telepathic contact would stretch only a short distance, a quarter kilometer or so. They could draw near to one another by gauging the increasing or decreasing strength of their own ability to communicate telepathically.

Come to me, brothers and sisters, thought Slider

Dan. *Don't be afraid. This is not a catastrophe. It is an opportunity. This is a chance to go where none of the people have gone before.*

But we're going to die, said Missile-in-Rock, who, true to her namesake, was a very quick borer, but she had been shy and timid in personality when dealing with other Horta. She was not of Slider Dan's clan but was of the Sand Blaster Clan. This did not trouble Slider Dan. He had always felt that his being a Horta was more important than his clan affiliation, and now he sensed this truth even more profoundly. Yet his own clan, the Tunnel Borers, remained extremely meaningful to him, as one is proud of a birthplace or place of schooling. One of the others was of the Sand Blaster Clan and the other was of the Melter Clan.

None of that mattered now. If one considered the odds, it was probable that they would be floating here forever. How long *could* a Horta live in space? They would perhaps be the first ever to find out. They would be the pioneers who knew the answer. Perhaps they would never be able to communicate this answer, perhaps they would.

The future was entirely uncertain—although the physical discomfort he was beginning to feel now was probably telling him something.

And then another thought occurred to Slider Dan: Was there a *reason* he and these others had been sucked out together, a greater meaning?

No. There could not be.

But perhaps there was a chance for a greater meaning. Perhaps he could *make* it mean something that they found themselves together.

Why not? When this was over they would have shared something that no other Horta had shared.

Space, the final frontier.

Let us try to move closer together, Slider Dan thought to the others. *This is the only way we will form a hive mind with so few of the people present. Let's attempt a simple formation.*

What? We're stranded out here, and you want us to fly around as if we were on recreational leave? thought the Horta from the Melter clan.

That is exactly what I believe we should do, Slider Dan replied. *Not for the sake of entertainment, although it will be entertaining, but for the sake of maintaining your sanity.*

I feel like I have indigestion—this is probably the effect of the vacuum. Furthermore, what you propose seems insane to me, said Missile-in-Rock. *But then all options seem insane at the moment.*

That's the spirit! replied Slider Dan. *Let us try something crazy, then. Let us try to move about by expelling the cut-juice from our underbellies. The All Mother has taught us that for every action there is an equal and opposite reaction. I did not truly understand what she meant at the time, but it seems as if this might be a good time to try the theory in practice and experience it for ourselves.*

They did just that, experimenting with expelling bits and pieces of their self-generated cutting solution from their undercarriages. They discovered that they need not expend much mass, only the equivalent of a few pellets ejected—but with the rail gun–like speed the Horta were capable of generating, it was enough to move them closer together. The telepathic field grew stronger among them. They were doing it. And moving through space felt almost . . . natural. Like sliding through rock.

Could it be that the people are made for space? thought Slider Dan.

Let us try a crystalline arrangement, say a pentagon, Slider Dan enjoined them. *There are five of us, let us form five points and see how we do.*

After a few miscues and mistakes, that is exactly what they did.

Now let us determine if we can rotate, Slider Dan continued, the urgency in his formed thoughts pushing them on.

And it worked. The Horta formation began to spin. The hive mind grew stronger and stronger among them the more they interacted. And there was a point when this hive mind grew stronger than the lines that separated them as clan members. There was a point when they became as one.

And in that moment, a new clan was born.

They didn't have to discuss the matter of what the clan would be named. The answer came to them at once in their deeply connected reverie.

The Star Clan.

On the bridge, Pavel Chekov was busy tracking down every last Horta that had been pulled out of the shuttle bay hatch and beaming those Horta back aboard. This took much longer than the captain liked, but space is vast, and although the *Enterprise*'s sensors were very powerful, it was like looking for a needle in a haystack.

Even more fortunate was the fact that when small bodies fell from subspace, they did so in dribs and drabs, as it were. There was a buildup until enough mass pressed against the space-time boundary, and then the dump into Newtonian space happened all at once. This meant that most of the Horta had dropped within a few kilometers of one another, and within that tiny space they were distributed in even smaller clumps of three to five.

Fortunately these groups were the equivalent of a very hot needle in a very cold haystack, so thermal long-range sensors proved to be effective, and the Horta were located down to the last one.

Toward the end of Operation Horta Overboard, as Kirk had heard Chekov name it sotto voce to Sulu, Spock reappeared on the bridge. He reported that the saved Horta were being reintegrated into the crowd in the shuttle bay, and that there were many Horta equivalents of tearful reunions.

"The speaker of the Horta, the one I communicated with most effectively before, Slider Dan, is still among the missing. Do we have a report on any remaining Horta in space?" asked Spock.

"Our sensor tally and the Horta's own count of their missing members match up," said Chekov. "We'll be in range to beam aboard the last five Horta within minutes."

"That includes Slider Dan," said Spock. "Captain, I suggest that we meet him in the transporter room and welcome him back aboard. The other Horta listen to him. He is the most individualistic of them, and the Horta with whom I have the greatest rapport. His mind is very strong and strategically oriented. In fact, it reminds me of another mind, one I have come in contact with in the past."

"Who is that?" asked Kirk.

"You, Captain," said Spock.

Kirk accompanied Spock to the transporter room, and they were standing by when Slider Dan was beamed aboard. He had a crust of what must be frozen atmosphere on his carapace, but he immediately began shuffling about in a Horta-like fashion after he materialized.

Spock established a mind meld immediately. This was becoming an easy procedure with practice.

There was, of course, the danger that he might at some point be absorbed into the Horta group mind and not be able to extract himself. But the Vulcan had found that the telepathic link that he shared with the Horta was much more casual and superficial than the more profound link he shared with other Vulcans, and yet not so much the jarring experience he'd experienced mind melding with the utterly alien.

"Spock, please express my regret about what's happened, and ask them if they're all right," Kirk said.

Spock relayed the question and Slider Dan, after a moment's hesitation, was able to answer in a sprightly manner that might have included a chuckle were it spoken aloud. *Hail, Spock! I am fine. Do not worry yourselves in that regard.*

"He reports that he is doing well, Captain."

"Very good. Tell him that we have tracked down one of the miscreants who sabotaged the shuttle bay hatch and that we will see that justice is done. When he has had time to rest, I will consult him and the other Horta upon this matter."

Spock passed along the thought, wordlessly.

Speaker from the Stars, tell your captain that I am none the worse for wear, and that I was able to remain in contact with several of my fellow clan members. While we were floating in space, we found that we could use the effluvia of our undersides as reaction mass and fly about in any manner we chose.

We expected rescue, or at least we had hopes for it, and we thought that the best use of our time was to enjoy ourselves while we were floating in the vastness of the galaxy. This also took our thoughts off the pressure discomforts. Such an opportunity will probably never come again, and we wished to make the most of it. That we did. We flew in formation, we flew separately, and we attempted various tricks and maneuvers. This we did to occupy ourselves and keep ourselves from worrying overmuch about rescue. In short, we had a wonderful time, and we believe that space may be in our future, at least for some of us.

I am glad to hear this, Spock thought. *Perhaps you will also now be in a position to rethink your offer to me to become your new All Mother. You understand that I feel the same way about space exploration as you now do. Vulcans lack many emotions, but we are filled with a burning curiosity, and there is nothing like seeking out new worlds and new civilizations to fulfill that need.*

The Horta was silent for a moment, and then in Spock's mind the thought of total understanding coalesced.

We would like to present a new clan to you, Speaker from the Stars.

Fascinating, thought Spock. *Please do so.*

Here is the Star Clan, Slider Dan intoned in thought. *We are your children, Speaker from the Stars*

"What's going on, Spock?" asked Kirk. "What are you two thinking?"

"We are coming to an understanding," said Spock. "Our similarities are greater than our differences, and I believe both myself and the Horta truly understand this now. They are a remarkable species. And it would be an honor to become the new All Mother, should that ever come to be."

"You're seriously considering this?" asked Kirk

"Not really, Captain," said Spock. "But, as I believe the saying goes: It *is* an honor to be nominated."

Rescuing the Horta proved to be challenging, but now every last one of the castaways was collected. Kirk and Spock accompanied Slider Dan back to the shuttle bay, and there they met McCoy, who had been standing by to check out all incoming Horta and to treat any ailments from vacuum or extreme cold.

"I told you before," said McCoy. "I'm a doctor, not a veterinarian or construction worker. What I don't know about these creatures' physiology could fill volumes."

"And I told you before," said Kirk, "you're a healer, so heal."

"Well, the truth is, as far as I can tell, I'm not needed here," McCoy grumbled.

In the shuttle bay, the several hundred Horta who had not been spaced were gathered in a large circle around those who had. Spock quickly touched a Horta and joined in the common mind meld of the creatures. He reported back that what was going on was a storytelling session.

"They seem to possess the resiliency of teenagers," said Spock. "They're not fazed by change and uncertainty the way an older creature might be. I don't know whether to attribute this to the species itself or to their relative youth."

"Or to both," Kirk said.

"Quite," replied Spock. "In any case, I do not believe the doctor's services will be required on this occasion."

"Thank the powers that be for little favors."

"I don't know what I was going to do if they *had* needed my help," muttered McCoy. "I filled up that phaser wound on the All Mother with thermo-concrete. This time I thought I may have to coat them in hot tar or something equally bizarre."

"Thank you, Doctor," Kirk said to McCoy's retreating back. "Spock, the Horta are not even the slightest bit upset by this mishap?"

Spock shook his head. "They are concerned about their safety. And when they experienced the loss of the castaways, it was as if a wound had opened up in their collective mentality. It is hard to express in terms a human would understand, but it is as if you experienced a sudden amputation of an extremity. The loss was felt in an almost physical sense. Now that the missing Horta are returned and reconnected to the group mind, there is a sense of rejoicing and happiness, and, most of all, of completion. While I cannot share in their joy, I sense its presence. It is a feeling of profound relief on their part."

"Better than profound anger," said Kirk. "All right, we've heard from our returned Horta, but what did they *do* while they were waiting to get picked up?"

"As I understand it from Slider Dan, the Horta are capable of producing reactionary ejecta from carapaces. They were able to experiment with various maneuvers. As we discovered, groups fell out very near together, and, while they were frightened that they would not be rescued, as sensible creatures they decided to make the most of the situation. They began flying about together, conjoining in formations. Furthermore, they looked around and took in all they could of the sky—something they almost never see on Janus VI. For some of these Horta, the experience was extremely moving, verging on sacred. And they want more of it."

"When the job is done," Kirk said.

"Yes, I believe they understand this," Mister Spock answered.

Kirk smiled. It was as he suspected. Once a

sentient species experienced the wonder of space flight, they seldom wanted to give it up. And some among them would always yearn for it thereafter. The Horta were no different than humans in this respect. It wasn't inconceivable that a Horta might become a Starfleet officer, as a matter of fact. Maybe even a captain.

That was the future. For now, Vesbius was one day away at warp eight. The asteroid was drawing closer and closer. There was no guarantee that Spock's and Scotty's plan would work. The captain was sure that it could be modified along the way. But time was pressing and there was little room for error. This one would be close—and a world and its people hung in the balance.

Twelve

Sulu sat back from the computer screen in his quarters and shook his head in dismay. The history of the Deneb II brush wars was an extremely unsavory and disheartening subject for research, and he'd spent a couple of hours immersed in it. Both sides in the conflict had behaved abysmally, and this was compounded by the fact that the ideologues on both sides had defined the other as inhuman.

The planet surface became a mosaic of nanotech-driven insanity, terrible transformation, and total destruction. Whole swaths became uninhabitable, filled with dueling nanotech-animated zombie armies in perpetual, preprogrammed struggle with one another. Humans who ventured into such areas entered a killing zone out of a surrealist nightmare.

That had been Merling's training ground, thought Sulu. No wonder he had turned out to be such a troubled soul.

But what did any of this have to do with the current mission?

Sulu was not sure, but something did not smell

right, and he was determined to get to the bottom of it.

To do so, he had enlisted the aid of Chekov and the ship's interior sensors. He was expecting the ensign at any minute.

Sulu ordered up hot water and was preparing to make himself a cup of tea when Chekov arrived. "Come in." The door to his quarters slid open and the Russian ensign entered. He saw Sulu's teapot and his eyes lit up.

"Is that the special blend your grandmother sent you?"

"It is," said Sulu. "Would you like a cup?"

"Don't mind if I do," Chekov replied. Without waiting to be invited, Chekov pulled up a chair and sat down across from Sulu at the cabin's small worktable. Sulu didn't mind. After three and a half years of working together, he and Pavel had become close friends and had saved each other's lives more than once. Neither stood on ceremony.

Sulu carefully placed the tea in the cup and poured hot water over it. This tea was *matcha*, the thick tea his grandmother used in her ceremonies, and it was wonderfully rich. Sulu liked to carry his own supply of tea. After Sulu carefully mixed the tea he nodded. Chekov took a sip and sighed in contentment.

"My compliments to your grandmother," he said. "So, how did your research go?"

"Deneb II," said Sulu, shaking his head. "What a sad story."

"A civil war?"

"Yes, a terrible one," Sulu answered. "The worst part about the conflict was that the humanoid government and rebels were not merely from the same background, but were blood relations in many cases. None of that seemed to matter once the fighting started."

"And what were they fighting over?"

"Water," said Sulu. "Plain water."

Sulu explained further that at issue had been rights to the planet's limited fresh water supply. For a century, wells were owned and controlled by certain families. But after the Federation discovered the planet, and despite the Prime Directive, the outside world trickled in as the locals sought to adopt modern ways of doing things. The trouble was, what was modern on Deneb II turned out to be centuries out of date within the larger Federation.

Eventually, the planetary government, never strong to begin with, divided into two factions. The Water Holders were those who still believed in family rights to wells. But they took it a step further and proclaimed that individual well water must *only* be drunk by the family that owned it.

The Water Sharers, on the other hand, believed in communal ownership of all wells. Upkeep of wells, which was a continual nuisance on Deneb II with its frequent choking sandstorms, was to be a task all must help with. In Sharer territories, instead of everyone keeping the wells clear, no one did. The Sharers blamed the Holders for their bad wells, and the Holders believed the Sharers sacrilegious polluters who drank unpurified water and had turned into demons as a result.

When war broke out, it was ugly, for by this time, both sides had used the planet's considerable wealth from dilithium mining to purchase advanced weaponry. Those weapons had all come with contingents of "advisors."

Chekov sipped his tea. "This is all very interesting, but what does it have to do with our Major Merling?"

"Let's cut to the chase," Sulu said. He finished his own tea and continued the tale.

"Johan Merling had been one of those outside advisors. After serving an extremely undistinguished stint in his homeworld's militia, Merling had put himself on the market as a mercenary and had ended up on Deneb II as advisor to the Sharer government. His expertise was in unconventional warfare, and, according to official records, Merling had trained a special forces unit whose mission was to poison Holder wells and knock them out of commission as water sources.

"I followed the trail easily enough to this point, but then things get murky," Sulu said. "Merling disappears from the official records as Deneb II descended from rebellion to chaos to complete collapse."

"Perhaps those records were altered?" Chekov offered.

"It's more likely all the record keepers were killed," said Sulu.

"And Merling had a hand in killing them?"

"Possible," Sulu answered. "In any case, the Holder faction seemed to have the upper hand for a time, but the Sharers resurged. They consolidated their power, and a mass execution of Holders was begun. What started as a war became genocide. Then, as the Holders fought back in desperation, out came the forbidden military nanotech."

"And you think it was Merling? Cossack!"

Sulu nodded in agreement. "No one knew if it was the Sharers or the Holders who struck first, but someone dropped nano into the wells. The restricted military nano spread and destroyed all in its path, as if the very world had caught the plague. An infected well was literally turned to a poisonous jelly. Those who drank from it died writhing in pain, and then their bodies became infected, zombie-like 'walkers' that traveled about spreading the contagion." Sulu sat back and shook his head. "That's all I have, however. All circumstantial evidence, I'm afraid."

"Perhaps I can bring us up to date." Chekov

finished his tea and then raised his data slate. "I have some interesting findings to report."

That was Chekov—a man made for easy enjoyment but able to turn on a dime to full engagement if the situation called for it. Sulu appreciated these qualities in his friend. Sulu was not so much a master of relaxation as he was a man with hobbies, many hobbies. He had caught the collecting bug at a young age and used it to alleviate the tension of his duties, ensuring the safety of the ship. He had an interest in weaponry long before he'd become a weapons officer himself, and he had an interesting assortment.

"What have you discovered?" Sulu asked his friend.

"First, I examined corridor playback during the shuttle bay incident," Chekov said. "Our Major Merling was nowhere near the shuttle bay or the Horta while on the ship except for one brief visit, where he'd been accompanied by Captain Kirk, Hannah Faber, and her aides. What's more, Bellamy Hox definitely *did* slip away for a moment during that tour. Hox probably planted the nano in the control room then."

"We know Hox is guilty of attempted murder. When he wakes up from that phaser stun, we'll find out more, I'm sure. But we've got nothing on Merling?" Sulu asked. His instincts told him Merling was somehow involved.

"I didn't say that," Chekov replied with a smile. Sulu filled his cup again, and Chekov took another sip of tea.

"Well, go on," said Sulu, keeping the impatience from his voice. You didn't get anywhere from ordering Chekov about when he was off duty. According to Pavel, nobody could ever be more harsh and dictatorial than his own father, and he considered those who tried to lord it over him only pale imitations of his old man.

The ensign set his teacup back down. He held up a plastic computer card. "The log record for personal locker 57A."

"Enlighten me," Sulu said.

"Since Merling didn't want to be anywhere near Spock or the Horta, we had to put him on deck eight in the technician and ensign berths. As you know from your days down there, *Lieutenant,* these are not the roomiest of spaces. Major Merling beamed up with personal luggage that had to be stored elsewhere."

"In personal locker 57A," Sulu said.

"Exactly," replied Chekov. He slid the card into his computer and the two watched a speeded-up recording of the locker's access record. Merling came several times to the locker and each time was careful to open it only when no one else was in the corridor. Sometimes this required waiting a good ten minutes. Privacy was more important than quick access, it seemed.

"The interesting point is coming up," Chekov said. His hand hovered over the control button on the monitor. "Here," he said, and he pressed the button, freezing the display.

Merling's hand was just coming out of the locker, holding something. "Can we zoom in on what he's got there?" Sulu asked.

"Certainly," said Chekov. He framed and zoomed the image to the item in the major's hand.

The enlargement showed an instrument with silver trimming on a coal-black body. He'd seen something like this before. Sulu studied it closer. It had a splayed muzzle-like area on the front that was colored bright red, as if to mark the dangerous end.

Sulu's collector instinct awoke. He was looking at a weapon of some sort. But from where did he know this?

Deneb II. He'd briefly considered what it would be like to own one of those weapons for his collection—discharged and decommissioned, of course.

"A little more, down where he's gripping it."

Chekov obliged, and the enlarged image came into focus. And there it was.

"The maker's mark," said Sulu. "Rendar Armory. See the curly silver *R* there with the numeral *7* beside it?"

"I do," Chekov said. "But what is it?"

"That, my friend, is a military nanotech injector pistol," Sulu said. "A Rendar Mark 7. They were outlawed fifty years ago. The only contemporary use on record was a decade ago—on a troubled little planet called Deneb II."

"Merling has outlawed weaponry," said Chekov. "We must arrest him."

Sulu smiled and put a hand on Chekov's shoulder. "We must confront him. We have no evidence other than my hunch."

"You *are* an expert in such matters," Chekov replied.

"Thank you," Sulu said. "But for now, let's go have a talk with Major Merling in his quarters, shall we?"

"Absolutely."

"And bring your tricorder," Sulu added. "We may be able to sniff out any nanotech in the area, even if it's deactivated."

They took the turbolift to deck eight and were walking down the corridor when Chekov's tricorder pinged. They paused as Chekov checked the readout.

"Nanotech?" asked Sulu.

"No," Chekov replied. He turned a knob and pressed a button to switch modes. "This is strange."

"What is it?"

"I am picking up subspace transmissions. On a very low frequency. We would normally not

monitor it on the ship, but since nanotech programming can be triggered by a subspace signal, I had it
set to receive."

"Is it a trigger signal?"

"No, it's modulated," said Chekov. "A message."
He popped up another readout. "It's coded."

"Can you break the code?"

Chekov examined the device screen. "It seems
to be an older code, and the key is in the database."

The two stood in the corridor while Chekov
adjusted his tricorder. A few curious faces passed
them by, but Sulu just smiled and waved them
along.

"Yes, I have it," said Chekov.

A tinny voice arose from the tricorder, soft in
volume, but unmistakably Major Merling's.

*"Yes, I understand. But the bombs did their work.
The tunnels are unusable."*

Another, harder voice from the other end. It was
a man's voice, and it seemed to drip with cynical
disdain. *"Now they scramble for this new solution.
We can never count on the idiots to do what they
must. All hope must be lost for a general evacuation
to be ordered."*

*"Many will die. The vaccines do not work beyond
a few days."*

"The strong will adapt," said the voice. *"Vesbius
must fall, or there can be no progress."*

"Yes, yes, I do agree," Merling replied.

"*The Federation ship must not arrive. These creatures must not pollute our system. You must see to it. Are you strong?*"

"*I am strong,*" Merling replied.

"*Then do your duty. For yourself and for Exos.*"

A pause, then a quiet mumbled reply: "*I will obey.*"

Chekov looked at Sulu. "Looks like your hunch has become proof."

"Let's get in there!" said Sulu.

They rushed to the door using Sulu's weapons officer override and burst through into the cabin.

There was no one in Merling's quarters.

"What is going on?" said a bewildered Chekov. But there on a desk sat the answer: a large metallic cylinder. Sulu picked it up. "A transceiver relay," he said. "Too big to carry about. This unit is the primary sender and receiver, however. Merling must have a portable unit with him. Can you trace it?"

Chekov already had his tricorder working on the problem. "I am getting a faint carrier signal." He looked up in surprised concern. "From engineering, access tube D."

"Isn't that—"

"Life support," Chekov said. "But Merling is confined to this deck."

Sulu got security on the way, but that would take time. He considered. "Aren't we close to engineering?"

"Yes," Chekov replied. "The ensigns complain of the vibrations all the time when they are trying to sleep, although it has never bothered me."

"That tube is vertical. There ought to be an access to a Jefferies tube on this deck." Sulu ran down the corridor. "Here."

The tube was sealed with a hatch. This was nothing a phaser couldn't handle, and Sulu had brought his along—just in case. He was about to blast the latches when he noticed that they were already loose. Someone had come this way, and recently.

Pulling the hatch off, Sulu climbed inside the Jefferies tube. Chekov was about to follow. "Get security to meet me in engineering," he said. "We've got to stop him. I'll do what I can. You come at him from below."

Chekov hesitated for a moment. Sulu could see that he didn't want to let his friend go into the tube alone, but he turned to find an intership communicator panel. Sulu began climbing down the ladder.

Below him, he heard more muttering. "Shaft A or B? Damn these schematics. I'll infect them both."

This was all Sulu needed to hear. He launched himself from the ladder and shot straight down through the tube. His feet connected with something solid, then pounded into the relative softness of a head and shoulders, and Sulu felt the shudder of contact travel throughout his body. There was a startled cry of pain, and then Sulu continued falling—now entangled with another.

There was a thud as the two reached the bottom of the tube. This entrance was to the Jefferies tube and was not covered with a hatch. The two rolled out of the tube and on to the deck of main engineering. Mister Scott was surprised to see them.

"Mister Sulu, what are you—"

But Merling recovered first. He shook Sulu off like a wild man, then scrambled around until he saw the weapon he had dropped and yanked it up. It was the Rendar Mark 7 Sulu had recognized.

"Back off!" Merling yelled, pointing the red muzzle at Scott and Sulu. Sulu pulled himself to his feet just in time to stop Scotty from charging at the major.

"He's got a nano weapon there, Mister Scott," Sulu said. "It can be deadly."

"Damn right." Merling stalked over to the main engineering panel and placed the muzzle against it. "All I have to do is pull this trigger, and your ship and all those aboard . . . die."

Chekov rushed in with two red-shirted security officers wielding phasers.

"Wait," called Sulu. "Nano." They stopped in their tracks. Even after being outlawed for years, the threat of military nanotech was enough to scare anyone.

"Don't you see, this didn't have to happen?" said Merling.

Yes, keep him talking, Sulu thought. *Keep his finger from pulling that trigger.*

"If you people hadn't shown up with your ship and your plans, we had everything in place to save them all."

"They are trying to save themselves."

Merling shook his head sadly. "Sheep. Genetically enhanced sheep hiding in their underground sheep pens. But the next step, a necessary step, to what we are about to become as a species. We must set the wolf upon them. Selection must take place."

"And you're the wolf?"

"Exos," said Merling. "That is our purpose."

"You're willing to kill children, to kill an alien species that did you no harm?"

Merling shrugged. "I learned on Deneb II an important lesson," he said. "Sometimes you must be cruel to be kind." He shook his head sadly. "It's a thankless task, but future generations will be grateful."

"I wouldn't count on that," Sulu said. And then the lieutenant noticed something: The Rendar 7's casing was cracked, probably from the fall. "Major, if I were you, I'd be very careful—"

Sulu took a step forward.

With a snarl, Merling pulled the trigger on the device.

Nothing happened.

He pulled it again, with the same result. Then he raised the weapon to look at it.

That was when Merling knew: The nano had leaked. Merling screamed in fear and attempted to toss the weapon away. No good. His hand was now fused to the handle. In fact, it was impossible to tell flesh and weapon handle apart.

And then the melting effect began to travel up Merling's arm.

"No!" he screamed.

He turned to Sulu, a look of abject horror on his face. "Help me," he said.

Sulu slowly shook his head and backed away. He turned to the security officers. "Phasers on full," he said to them. Both quickly followed orders.

"Please, it's . . . I can feel it . . . eating me alive," Merling said. He tried to take a step forward, but his legs only moved slightly, as if they were made of hot wax. His entire body was quickly losing its form, turning to primordial goo. Dangerous goo, should it get loose on the ship. It could eat through decks, walls. And if this were the Deneb II master strain, it could turn the entire crew into the shambling dead.

"Fire phasers!" Sulu ordered.

A sheet of power took Merling's collapsing form and surrounded it with phased energy. After a momentary flicker, Merling and the nano were broken down to invisible elemental gas.

"Ugh, what's that smell?" Scotty said.

"Sulfur in the nano," Sulu said. "Harmless now."

"Not to my nose," Mister Scott replied.

And despite the circumstances, his aching ankles from landing on Merling, and the near-miss encounter with destruction, Sulu had to smile a weary smile.

Thirteen

Captain's log, Stardate 6415.1. Through industrious research and legwork, Lieutenant Hikaru Sulu and Ensign Pavel Chekov discovered and thwarted a plot by Vesbian military attaché Major Johan Merling to use forbidden nanotechnology to destroy this ship. Merling's attempted sabotage was only incidental to a plot to obliterate the Horta currently aboard Enterprise. *His plan was to force a mass exodus of the planet Vesbius in order to forward the genetic supremacist views of a Vesbian organization, Exos, to which he secretly belonged. Commendations are recommended for Misters Sulu and Chekov.*

The *Enterprise* blazed into the Vesbian system at warp eight and did not slow down until it had reached the orbital plane of the outer planet. Then, using a combination of faster than light and impulse power, the ship maneuvered into orbit around the oncoming asteroid. The first deployment of the Horta to the asteroid's surface was overseen by Spock and Scott.

The Horta arranged themselves in an ant-like double line and made their way through the *Enterprise*'s corridors to the transporter room. When they had to enter the turbolifts they waited patiently. Rather than depending on a human operator being always present, Scotty had created a Horta-friendly command handle located in the bottom of the lift the Horta would be using. Unlike the human-centric turning handle, this was a toggle-switching device that could be pressed against to activate. The destination was preset, since all the Horta were going to the transporter room.

Spock, with Scotty's input on engineering matters, had prepared careful instructions and communicated them to the Horta on what they were to do once they deployed on the asteroid. The *Enterprise* had conducted extensive external scans, and the asteroid was now mapped to a centimeter resolution. The Vulcan studied the readouts carefully and created what he told the captain was a mental map similar to the smell map used by a Terran canine or other chemical-sensing creature. This map would represent the layout of the asteroid to the Horta.

"I informed them of chemical concentrations, of regions of ice and rock, and the density layers to the depth to which our sensors could penetrate," Spock explained. "These are things that Horta understand instinctively. They are remarkably quick at assimilating the information. It was as if I were telling a Vulcan, who already knew, the way to Shi'Kahr."

The Horta marched into the transporter room and were beamed down to the asteroid to meet Scott. He had previously beamed down in an EV suit to where a promising crack lay that might provide ingress to the asteroid's interior. Within the space of a few hours, the Horta had dug into the asteroid and gone to work. The overall plan was to create weaknesses necessary for the destruction of the asteroid, but to do so in a precise manner. After that, the *Enterprise* would use her tractor beams and phasers to complete the job. Before the *Enterprise* went into action, the Horta would gather in a prearranged spot on the asteroid's surface and be beamed back aboard.

It was a complex operation, something that only a species that was capable of long-range planning and thinking could even conceive of completing. Kirk was more and more impressed with the Horta the longer he was in contact with them. They were not merely intelligent, but advanced. He would, without question, author a report supporting Federation membership.

Would the plan work? Spock believed that it would, and Scotty had become increasingly optimistic about its chances for success. But there were many unknowns. For despite all the scans the

Enterprise had completed of the asteroid, there were many uncharted regions the Horta would encounter. In some places, they might need sensors. Mister Scott offered to remain on the asteroid with the Horta to provide backup and assistance.

The only reason the plan had a chance to succeed was the fact that the asteroid was a combination of a nickel-iron asteroid and a comet. The metallic interior was all asteroid, but either through accretion or collision—Spock thought it had been the latter—the asteroid core had accumulated a rock and ice outer coating. Finally, the rind of the asteroid, its surface, was made up of more common silicon debris to depths of ten to fifteen meters, Spock estimated from millennia of strikes from micrometeorites.

If everything went exactly as expected, when the asteroid entered the outer reaches of Vesbius's gravitational well, and with the proper assist from the *Enterprise,* the asteroid would break apart; the greater part of its mass would miss the planet, and only meteors would strike the surface. The meteor storm would be bad, potentially harmful, but not utterly devastating to the biosphere of the planet.

With the Horta and Mister Scott deployed on the asteroid, the *Enterprise* headed toward Vesbius at warp speed and was soon in orbit. As they drew near to her homeworld, Hannah became stronger. It was as if her body could sense the approaching planet, or perhaps the effect was merely psychological. When Kirk accompanied her from sickbay to the transporter room to beam down, there was a look of elation and relief in her eyes. She was so gaunt that she seemed ethereal to Kirk, only a shadow of the girl he'd met weeks before. If she were an angel returned to her heaven, it was a heaven Kirk could only visit, where he could never remain. For living there required giving up not only being human, but something even more important: his command.

Kirk and Spock accompanied Hannah and Ferlein to the surface of Vesbius, along with a security detail. Spock could answer any questions about Operation Horta that the Council might have. The security detail was there to accompany their prisoner, Hox.

The captain wanted to hold on to Hox, but it was clear that if he did so Hox would die. Kirk negotiated an agreement that Hox would be guarded by *Enterprise* security until he was handed over to the Vesbian police. The chancellor assured the captain that every measure would be taken to ensure that an Exos compatriot did not liberate Hox.

But Hox was among the least of Kirk's worries. On Vesbius, ten percent of families had decided to evacuate. These came to about two thousand people. This may have also been a reaction to the terrorist bombings. The tunnel bombs had collapsed two shelters, which was fully one third of the capacity, and five thousand people were without adequate protection from *any* strike, much less a full-on asteroid hit.

There was no way two thousand people could fit on the *Enterprise* for even a single trip. The original plan had been to make several trips to ferry the colonists to nearby systems for permanent resettlement and, most tellingly, to accompany and protect what was assumed to be a vast evacuation flotilla. At the moment, that flotilla consisted of the *Enterprise* and a motley collection of planetary shuttlecraft and merchant haulers.

There was no life-support structure on Vesbius's airless moons. Furthermore, there was no solution to the problem of autoimmune collapse. The only real hope was to take to space, avoid the strike, and then return in the hopes of finding some scrap of the biosphere left to interact with their Vesbian biological equilibrium. Despite the obvious flaws and huge uncertainties in the plan, Kirk ordered every shuttle the *Enterprise* had available to take part in the evacuation effort that was under way.

The day after the *Enterprise*'s return, knowing all that he could do now was wait, the captain beamed down to spend a night with Hannah. On the dawn of the following day, they chose the veranda where they had met for a goodbye. Everything now depended on operational issues neither could foresee, and both were acutely aware that this might very well be the last time they saw one another. Standing together with a view of the verdant fields of the Vesbian colony, the quaint farmhouses, the cobblestone roads, the distant snowcapped mountains, it was almost impossible to imagine that all of this might be gone within days.

"I'll try to remember what it was like," said Hannah. "The memory fades. Yet I believe that if I hold it in my heart, I will someday be able to re-create this for my children or for their children's children. That is my hope."

"Our plan could succeed," said Kirk. "The Horta might be successful. They are very resourceful."

"If by a miracle the salvation does come," Hannah said, "I will treat it as a gift, and I will cherish every day that I live on my beautiful world ever after. I will never take this life for granted." She turned to Kirk, smiled, and touched his lips. "I am not so very unlike a human woman, am I? I am not so very unlike someone you might love?"

There was so much that he might have said, should have said, but Kirk, so often the master of such situations, found himself at a loss. His only response was to kiss her, and the kiss lasted for a long time.

Kirk stepped back. They did not exchange

another word. There was nothing left to say, nothing to take the sting from the moment.

"Kirk to *Enterprise*. One to beam up."

He gazed at Hannah as the transporter beam engulfed him. His last thought was that at least he'd had such a morning with such a woman.

The captain rode the turbolift in a contemplative mood, but as soon as he stepped on to the bridge, James Kirk knew *this* was right. Chekov had a report from the asteroid surface that the Horta were finding the asteroid crust harder than expected. If they could not find a way into the planetoid that was relatively easy and would not take weeks, the plan was in jeopardy of collapsing before it had even begun. Kirk called an emergency briefing to assess the situation. This was the life he had chosen, and, very slowly but very surely, Kirk's mood lightened.

This is where I belong, Kirk thought, smiling at the bustle about him as officers went about their duties with precision and creativity. *I made the right decision.*

Didn't I?

Fourteen

When the antimatter bombs went off, Scotty thought they made for a sensor reading to behold. Fortunately, he was on the other side of the asteroid and did not have to directly experience the cataclysm. The antimatter was loaded into strategic fissures in the asteroid surface, and the effects of the explosions were increased by at least an order of magnitude by placement. With a contained reaction explosive, the Horta were able to move in rapidly and clear the pulverized regolith out of the newly exposed passageway into the asteroid.

Exterior sensor scans from the *Enterprise* had revealed two fault structures that could be exploited. Scott had made three more incisions, as he liked to think of them, with photon torpedoes. These had turned an even smaller fault system into a cracked stretch of crustal plates resembling a hardboiled egg that had been dropped (but not peeled), and created a major weakness to exploit in the asteroid. Because of the odd structure of this asteroid, it shared many behaviors with worlds such as Earth or Vulcan, and had a limited version of plate tectonics in operation. The disadvantage to its being an asteroid was that the crust was exposed to space and a full pounding of micrometeorites over millions of years. This resulted in an outer coating compressed to diamond hardness. Without a way in, the Horta found they could not create the massive system of honeycombed fissures and chambers that the plan called for. Even if they eventually broke through, they wouldn't accomplish this within the time that they had remaining before the day of the possible strike.

But the photon torpedoes and antimatter explosions proved enough to give the Horta a foothold, and they were able to work into the cracks much more easily than they would have been able to without technological aid.

After the explosions were complete, Scott turned his attention back to his more mundane tasks—seismic sensory activity in his tunnel rover.

Scott had to admit he was having the time of his life. He'd taken a shuttle down to the asteroid surface and met the Horta there. In the shuttle was a scanning device he had constructed himself. It was similar in makeup to the old seismic trucks of Earth, the sensor vehicles that had traveled around Earth of the twentieth and twenty-first centuries and pounded the ground to find oil back in the ancient days of carbon energy sources. The principles were basically the same here: You dropped a heavy weight on the ground, and this set up waves of compression and decompression that traveled through the rock. Different densities of different portions of the regolith either slowed or allowed the compression wave to pass through at an average speed. The waves bounced about were directed back to Scott's sensor device and into vector angles of other devices that he had placed on the asteroid. The engineer was able to triangulate the information he received and construct a 3-D rendering of the asteroid. Furthermore, with the quantum capabilities of the subspace sensors, Scotty was able to refine these measurements, and he could predict not only the general consistency of the rock that would be found there but the particular crystallization patterns that the Horta would encounter. This was useful information to the Horta, akin to telling a sailor what the weather would be like each day on his voyage.

For his part, Scotty had very much come to respect the Horta as natural engineers. They made tunnels that would not collapse due to external pressure. This was a much harder feat than it might appear. One could not simply dig a hole to any depth one might desire in a planet or an asteroid. Pressure on the sides increased with depth. The need to overcome such pressure had been the bane of Earth drillers and miners for centuries. Using specialized teams, the Horta were able to physically

restructure the molecular bonds of the tunnel cas-
ings and shore up those spaces to an astonishing
depth and at almost incredible pressure. One Horta
team would cut through the rock, and a second
trailing team would shore up the tunnel behind the
lead. Then a third crew would come through and do
the finishing work of conducting a thorough crack
inspection along the way and sealing any stray
weaknesses. This method produced tunnels under
the surface that were precise.

*I can understand why the miners were reluctant
to part with the Horta, even for a few days,* Scotty
thought. *It's like having your own personal army
of engineers who can carve a tunnel that's stronger
and safer than anything that your tools could've produced.*

Scott had created a portable, tent-sized pressure
dwelling for himself on the asteroid, and his seismic sensor unit was housed in a two-seater buggy
that had a small atmospheric enclosure over the
driver and a passenger. The buggy was designed to
zip through the Horta tunnels using wheels on the
bottom and wheels on the top. Scott had to admit it
was fun to go tunnel-running at full speed. He took
to calling the vehicle Rover, and it did look a bit
like a sleek greyhound, with an extended nose that
housed the sensor apparatus.

Lacking the Vulcan's mind melding ability, Scott
had adapted the crude method of communicating

with the Horta that the Janus VI miners used. He often wondered what the Horta were really thinking. He was starting to get an idea that whatever it was, it was pretty complicated. These were sentient beings, and it became more and more apparent that they had their own opinions about life, the culture, and the universe.

They were clearly divided into groups that Scott quickly began thinking of as clans. This was something Scott both approved of and understood. After all, he was from a clan-based culture himself. He'd checked with Spock—who had proved helpful with his newly acquired personal trove of background data on Horta culture—and as near as Scotty could tell with his limited ability to communicate with the Horta, the different clans were *competing*. The prize for those who did the most work seemed to be a grant of proximity to the All Mother upon their return to Janus VI. Scott wished fervently that he could speak Horta; maybe one day he could find a way to do so.

The asteroid's amalgam of material was proving to possess an extremely complicated structure. The preliminary scans from the *Enterprise* had not distinguished the multitude of layers that made up this beast of an asteroid. A child of the gravitational effects of the two moons of Vesbius, the asteroid was a conglomeration of space debris the two moons had swept from Vesbian space and sent into a solar orbit. For millennia, the two moons had been very good at cleaning up and absorbing the blows from space that were aimed at Vesbius. This was important, since the planet was in the Goldilocks zone in the system: the perfect distance from the sun for water to exist in three phases at different times on the planet, and thus the right temperature and orientation for life to emerge.

Many planets were in the Goldilocks zone in the galaxy but held no life. Almost invariably, these were planets without moons. Now the double moons had caused the very problem they usually helped avert. It had taken a few million years, but the combined gravitation of Toro and Cabella, as the two moons were known locally, had pulled the asteroid off course. This had likely happened before in the planet's history, and it may have accounted for the fact that the life forms encountered on Vesbius had been relatively primitive, with plants akin to Mesozoic Earth ferns, rushes, and mosses. The colonists had introduced flowering plants, as well as a new dominant vertebrate species—*Homo sapiens*. If the planet was indeed a super organism, Scott was not surprised that the planetary ecosphere had not taken to humanity.

Scotty's short-range sensors told him that he was approaching the end of a tunnel and drawing near to a group of Horta who were lining it. He pulled the throttle back and slowed. Up ahead, the

Horta had sensed his arrival, probably via seismic waves traveling through the regolith, and were headed back to meet him. The leader—each group of four had one "foreman," generally—signaled Scotty through a series of wigwag maneuvers that were not unlike the dance movements of a honey bee, that they were preparing to evacuate the end of the tunnel so that Scott could go in and complete measurements for the next length of tunnel. Scotty used the rover to wigwag back the appropriate thank you, and he proceeded forward until the nose of the sensor brushed up against the tip end of the tunnel.

The rear of the tunnel rover was outfitted with a crane-like structure with a winch cable and a neutronic weight dangling on its end. The weight possessed a density nearly that of a thimble's worth of neutron star material, and even in the light gravitation of the asteroid, it oriented itself at all times toward the asteroid's center of gravity. Scotty deployed the antigrav crane to raise the heavy pounding device to the cocked position.

"All right, you Horta, better cover your ears or whatever it is you have, because I'm bringing the vibrations," Scotty said. He knew the Horta understood what was about to happen and would do just that. He toggled the electromagnetic rails that slammed the weight down—the wave-producing mechanism was basically a rail gun that he was firing into the asteroid's mass—and the resulting boom shook the little rover in its tracks. Scotty would be afraid of creating a cave-in in such circumstances had he not known of the skill with which the Horta made their tunnels. Nevertheless, bits and pieces of rock did break from the ceiling of the tunnel and rain down on his tunnel craft. The returning seismic wave registered almost instantaneously on Scott's instruments, and with that his measurement in this sector was done. He spun the rover seat around on a lazy Susan–like apparatus he had rigged and faced the opposite direction, up-tunnel and ready to travel back out.

Behind him, though, the Horta dig gang appeared to be blocking the tunnel. They stood in front of the rover and did not retreat, as they normally would, into the side tunnels they had constructed for that purpose. One of the Horta was moving up and down in such a manner that was almost humorous to Scotty's eyes, as if it were doing some sort of chicken dance. Scotty soon realized, however, that its purpose was serious, and that it was trying to signal him.

Now here's a problem, Scotty thought. *How am I gonna communicate with them after all our wigwag signals are exhausted?*

But it proved to be a simple message after all. Scotty had worked out seismic signals for very basic words. And the word the Horta group was thumping in unison was clear and distinct. They wanted something and they wanted it now.

We want Spock!

"I dinna know why they want you, Mister Spock," said Scotty over the subspace channel, "but it's very clear to me that they do. And what I thought was just a few Horta asking me is now a general request. In fact, I don't think they'll do much more work until they speak to you."

"Very well," said Spock. *"Did the Horta suggest a meeting place, or should I merely materialize on the planet's surface?"*

"They've hollowed out a resting area about half-way through the crust, a multisided chamber with lots of shallow depressions all around that I take to be more or less Horta bunk beds. I think that's probably the best place to make contact," replied Scott.

"Very well. I shall endeavor to answer their call," Spock replied. *"But this will take me away from critical readings on the planet surface that may give us clues as to the ability of the biosphere to survive."*

"Understood, Mister Spock," said Scotty, "but I don't think it can wait."

"I will consult with the captain and we should be able to warp within beaming range immediately. Spock out."

Well, I never heard that before, Scotty thought.

Mister Spock has all the signs of being very, very irritated by these bairns and their request.

A great many Horta were gathered in the resting area about five hundred meters below the surface of the asteroid. There was no appreciable gravity on the asteroid. As a consequence, Horta dotted the resting chamber like bees in a hive, with no one way being "up" or "down."

The chamber proved too deep for the transporter. Instead, Spock beamed down to the surface in an EV suit, where Scott and his tunnel rover met him. The Vulcan climbed aboard, and when the atmospheric bubble came down to cover them he was able to take off his helmet.

The trip down was an experience Spock would not soon forget. The engineer made full use of his rover's speed. Spock supposed the human would've found the ride great fun. Spock himself found it . . . efficient.

As the rover slowed, they emerged from the tunnel into the resting area. The engineer looked down at the sensors. "What the—" Scott spun around and looked behind him.

"What is it, Mister Scott?"

"The Horta. they've sealed up the way we came from." Scott turned back to his sensors. "And Mister Spock, can you beat this?"

"What?"

"I'm reading atmosphere out there. And pressure. They've managed to generate a Vulcan-like mix of atmospheric gases."

"Is the pressure of sufficient strength to exit this rover?"

"Aye, it seems to be, but I don't know if I would recommend—"

"Open the top up, Mister Scott," Spock said.

"Are you sure, sir?"

Spock considered. He needed full physical contact for a mind meld. Perhaps the Horta understood this and had prepared for it.

"I am," Spock replied. "Open the top on your rover, Mister Scott. I'm getting out."

"Aye, sir."

There was a pneumatic hiss, and then the thin Vulcan air that filled the chamber rushed in. Scott gasped for a moment before adjusting. For Spock, it felt like home.

Spock climbed out and with a push floated free of the rover. He did not possess enough mass to feel a gravitational effect within the asteroid.

A Horta approached and Spock removed one glove of his EV suit. He maneuvered into position to touch the Horta. Contact was immediately established—the Horta hive mind seemed to leap into being within Spock's awareness.

He had arrived in the midst of discussion and argument.

Welcome to the Conclave, Speaker from the Stars, thought the familiar individual voice of Slider Dan. *We have been awaiting your revered presence.*

And what may I do to aid you? Spock thought in return.

This requires some explanation, Slider Dan thought-spoke. *This rock is proving a harder chew than we first expected. It was very helpful for the human, Scott, to provide us with soft spots to latch on to, or we may never have found a quick and easy way into the heart of the rock.*

Mister Scott is a most excellent engineer, Spock thought in reply.

He will go down as a hero for our generation, and we shall remember him for ten thousand years, the Horta responded. *But now we have another problem—a problem that is likely beyond his ability to solve.*

What is that? asked Spock.

It is an issue that in the past only the All Mother could have resolved. You see, the caste system itself is in question at the moment. We Horta are born to different castes with specialized genomic strengths. There are the Hole Diggers and there are the Tunnel Borers, there are the Gem Collectors, and the People of the Blasting Sand. Each of these is also his own self, and yet very much a part of a clan. Our clans are not getting along at the moment.

It seems complicated, thought-spoke Spock, *but*

many societies have cultural differences and distinctions that they must deal with. You are young Horta. I have it on good faith from the All Mother herself that there is within each of you a collective memory that you must slowly learn to draw upon. This is exactly what the period of adolescence is for: to find your place within the Horta overmind, the part of your collective conscious that transcends the clan mind meld. Once you find that place as an individual, many of your group contentions will be resolved.

This may be true, Spock, but we have not found this overmind yet, and we do not have the All Mother with us. Here is the problem: The People of the Blasting Sand have a large disagreement with the Tunnel Borers. How this came about is difficult to pinpoint, but it was exacerbated when a group of Sand Blasters was relegated to the task of clearing away the detritus behind the Borers. The Borers believed it would be amusing to expel digestive waste products not into a privy tunnel—we usually cut these as side tunnels to our main excavations for just such a purpose—but to expel some waste products into the broken regolith that must be cleared. The Sand Blasters were surprised and disgusted to find these ejecta mixed with their usual burden. They refused to carry it away.

Are you telling me that one group decided to defecate into the workspace of the other group? asked Spock.

That is essentially the case. But the Sand Blasters,

*instead of merely taking this insult as a stupid prank,
allowed themselves to become offended for the honor of
their clan, and a group of them attacked the Borers. It
was a nasty fight. A great deal of rock was thrown and
a great many acid scars were imparted and received.*

*Sadly, one of our number has been seriously in-
jured as a result. More important, now the Tunnel
Borers and the People of the Blasting Sand are at an
impasse. They will not work together.*

Spock arched an eyebrow and nodded. *Will you
allow me to examine the one who is injured?* he said.

The gathered Horta moved to the side and revealed the injured one to Spock. It appeared, now
that he understood the sexual differences, to be a
large female. She had clearly been in a mishap; for
there were gaps in her carapace where rivulets of
the steaming ooze of magmalike interior fluid ran.

Spock bounced over to the Horta to examine
her. The female shuffled away at his touch for a moment but then was still.

Peace, Spock thought. *I seek only to aid you.*

The Horta seemed to understand. Spock drew
back and flipped open his communicator.

"Spock to *Enterprise.*"

"*Enterprise* here, Mister Spock."

"Please have Doctor McCoy beam down to the
asteroid," said Spock. "And tell him to bring with
him the exact bandaging material that he used during his mission to Janus VI."

"*Aye, sir, Mister Spock.*"

Spock waited for the hail he knew was coming. It did not take long. His communicator bleated, and Spock flipped it open. "Yes, Doctor McCoy?"

"*Well, you know it's me,*" said McCoy, "*so I guess you know why I called. Spock, I'm a doctor, not a construction worker. I have no idea why that thermo-concrete worked, and I have no idea if it will work again.*"

"Doctor, we have a wounded Horta here and she requires your assistance. You are the only experienced Horta physician in the Omega sector. As Captain Kirk said before: You are a healer, Doctor McCoy."

McCoy sighed. "*All right, Spock. I'll be right down.*"

Spock turned to Scott. "The matter seems urgent. This female Horta is in a great deal of pain. Will you link both our communicators in series, Mister Scott? I believe that will provide sufficient gain to provide a transporter lock for Doctor McCoy."

"Aye, give me a second." Spock handed the engineer his communicator and Scott quickly had the two linked on the same frequency. "Set."

"We're ready, *Enterprise*," Scott said. "Send the good doctor along now."

McCoy materialized with a bag of thermoconcrete and a bladder of water. Although movement was more difficult in the low-g cavern, with Scott's aid, McCoy began his work.

And now to the larger matter at hand, Spock thought to the Horta. *This clan contention must stop. We have no time to deal with such issues at the moment. It may be that the grievances on both sides are legitimate. The fact remains that this is not the time to seek retribution, or even justice, in this matter. We are at a critical phase of this operation. It must be completed. Many lives are in the balance. The pride of a particular clan, while very important, and perhaps even a necessary survival characteristic of your culture, must not take precedence over saving an entire population.*

We must protest, thought an unfamiliar voice within the hive mind. This was the voice of one of the Horta that Spock had not heard individually before. *We of the Sand Blasters must not stand in a lower ranking than the Tunnel Borers merely because they are better able to dig through rock. This ability does not mean that they are better in every way. Most of all, it does not mean that they should have a closer place to the All Mother! Since we are without the All Mother and you are the heir apparent, we wish to be made your honor clan. We see that the humans are more impressed with the showy Tunnel Borers, but there would be no holes that could be traversed without the clearing actions of the Blasters. We deserve to be your honor clan, and we will fight for the right.*

Am I to understand, thought Spock, *that the clans were ultimately fighting over* me? *That this has its roots in who will be* my *favorite?*

Slider Dan, Spock's usual contact, slid forward along a wall. By this point Spock was able to recognize him by the protuberances and markings of his exterior. The Horta thought-spoke within the hive mind, his voice resonant and distinct, somehow the most *individual* among the Horta.

Yes, Speaker from the Stars, that is the case, unfortunately. I am ashamed to say that we are perhaps not as advanced as you believe. Clans are fighting for status when the life of the world hangs in the balance. I am ashamed for us all, but it is better that we get this situation out in the open rather than hide it in dark tunnels where no one goes until it crawls out to bite us.

Spock turned to Scott and McCoy, who were busy treating the injured Horta of the Sand Blaster Clan. "Mister Scott, what would you do if you were presented with an argument among children, and the situation was such that you had to decide who was in the right, even when it seemed to you that no one was in the right? Or that there was no 'right' that might be determined?"

"Aye, that's the dilemma of all parents everywhere," Scott replied. "I don't care if they're Horta or Vulcan, Romulan, or Klingon. My old father would have said that you must make 'em understand that what they're fighting about doesn't matter a hill of beans to anybody else, and that it's going to get them in a world of trouble if they don't cut it out."

"Mister Scott, there is wisdom in what you've said," Spock replied. "In fact, it reminds me of a Vulcan proverb."

"What's that, Mister Spock?"

"Never cuddle with a *sehlat* until you can defeat it in battle."

Mister Scott slowly nodded his head. "Aye, I suppose if I understood that in the least, I would agree with you. One other thing, Mister Spock."

"Yes?"

"It might help if you give them something to . . . well, take their minds off their squabbles."

Spock nodded. It was an excellent suggestion. "Thank you," he said. "I now know what to do."

He turned back to the assembled Horta. *Here is a message from Speaker from the Stars,* Spock thought. *You ask me to decide which of the Horta clans I will place in a position of honor. That is, you inquired which of you I like better. The answer to this is that, as far as I am able, I like you all equally, and I respect and honor all of you each in your different way. That said, I must also point out to you that I am a Vulcan. Vulcans do not have emotions as you know them, and while I find you a curious and interesting species in many ways, I can never love you. I am simply incapable of doing this because of*

*my physiological makeup. Your All Mother loves you,
but I am not she. You must think of me more as your
All Father. My attitude toward all of you is one of
extreme emotional detachment.*

The Horta shuffled a bit as if a tremor of distress
had run through them. It could be that they had
never been spoken to in such a manner before. How
very unlike his own upbringing on Vulcan. Perhaps,
Spock considered, they were quite used to being
indulged by a loving All Mother with no corrective
whatsoever. After all, they lived on a resource-rich
planet with a caretaker who clearly doted upon
them all.

You must think of me not *as the All Mother,*
Spock intoned, *but as the All Father.*

How would his father, Sarek, put it? Spock wondered. He wasn't certain, but one thing he knew:
Sarek would speak logically and without mercy
or pity in the slightest, especially toward his own
children.

*And as your All Father, I say to you: it is time to
leave me to my work. It is time to go and find your
own way. Frankly, I have other things to do than to
come down here from my ship and settle your petty
differences. It may not occur to you, but I too have
to work. And I shall tell you something else: my
work gives me great satisfaction. I have no intention
of losing that satisfaction in order to placate your
wounded sense of clan honor.*

The Horta tremor became agitation. Horta shuffled back and forth within the chamber, and a grinding and rustling clamor of rock against rock arose. Spock decided to press his point home.

Now that you are away from your mother, Spock intoned, *it is incumbent upon you to find a way to handle your differences by yourselves. You must resolve your differences in a way that does not destroy your common purpose as well. But most of all, you must deal with your differences in a way that does not bother me. For, as I have explained, I have a great many matters that I must see to, and those matters are of great importance to your own place in this galaxy, and the future of Horta-kind in general. Make your peace now. The All Father demands it.*

The rumbling din within the chamber became a roar as Spock's thoughts made their way through the hive mind of the Horta.

It was Slider Dan who finally replied.

We wish to express our extreme apologies for having disturbed the All Father. We will find a way to overcome these differences among us without distracting you any further. What's more, the fact that you consider each Horta as equal in our own way had never occurred to most of us. It was our understanding that one of us had to be the honor clan, and so contention was built into all that we did. You have shown us a new way.

You did not need me to find this way, Spock thought. *It is fairly obvious and entirely logical. You each have separate strengths. Use them to make the whole greater, and not to tear the hive apart. And if you don't do so, I will have to impose the appropriate punishment.*

It was as if a collective gasp passed across the Horta now. *And what will that punishment be, All Father?*

Merely my extreme disappointment, said Spock. *I believe that that will sting you far more than any physical retribution I could employ. I will be very, very disappointed in you. You don't want that, do you?*

No! came the collective shout.

Then get back to work, said Spock, *and so shall I. And please don't make me come back down here.*

Never! But Speaker from the Stars . . .

Yes?

We . . . I have a suggestion.

I am listening.

Very well, thought Slider Dan. *Here is what I propose, All Father . . .*

Spock's mind flooded with their idea. The Vulcan paused to consider what had been put forward.

I will take this under consideration.

I believe it will work, Speaker from the Stars.

As I said, I will consider it and put it before the captain at the appropriate time. In the meantime, you must complete your task here and I must go to return to my duties.

Understood, Speaker from the Stars.

Spock grunted assent and broke his connection with the hive mind. He gazed around.

"So?" said McCoy. "Get your point across?"

"I have delivered the message," Spock said. "And you, Doctor McCoy?"

"I'll be damned if I haven't patched together another Horta," McCoy replied. "She may be sore for a while—who the heck knows?—but she will live to fight another day."

"Let us hope the internal struggles are over," Spock replied. "We haven't time for such nonsense."

The work of carving up the asteroid proceeded more smoothly thereafter, to Mister Scott's immense relief. With his tunnel rover's sensor apparatus showing the way, the Horta were proving to be the perfect workforce to exploit and build on its soundings. It seemed they were going to just pull it off.

The scoring cuts were being completed, but all would depend on four successive hammer blows from the ship's deflector shields and phasers to finish the process. All of the work would come to nothing if the calculations were not correct. The asteroid might break up, or it might not, but the deflector array would likely not be able to push the pieces out of a collision vector with Vesbius—they would either be too small or too large.

Nevertheless, Scotty found himself humming "The Bonnie Banks of Loch Lomond" as he worked with the Horta. Whatever the outcome, it was going to be one of the most glorious demolition projects in history, and he was happy to be the chief engineer on an undertaking of such epic scale. This was not because he wanted fame, but because Scotty felt he was putting his skills to their fullest possible use. And that was all a good engineer should ever want, in Scotty's estimation.

The work proceeded. The asteroid drew closer and closer to the planet.

It's going to be as close as close can be, Scotty thought. But he smiled when he considered the prospect, for with each passing hour he became more and more convinced that this harebrained scheme of Spock's might actually work.

Fifteen

Hannah Faber surveyed the motley collection of ships and lift vehicles that the settlement had assembled to aid the evacuees who were attempting to leave the planet before the asteroid arrived. When she had returned it had become apparent to all that repairs on the sabotaged underground shelters were not going to be completed in time. The Exos movement had not succeeded in its plan to destroy the structures entirely, but they may as well have, for they succeeded in making the shelters impossible to inhabit at the crucial moment they were needed. For all practical purposes, they may as well have collapsed the mountains on top of them.

This left five shelters that were inhabitable, each by three thousand people, if as many as possible were crowded in. With fifteen thousand of the settlement thus accounted for, this meant five thousand people must flee. There was no other choice. As the *Enterprise*'s Mister Spock might say, the logic was inescapable. They did not even address the problem of what would happen after the strike.

Once away, the evacuees could not remain in space or they would die just as surely as they would had they remained on the surface of the planet.

Hannah did hope that the Horta would succeed and the strike would be averted. But to plan on that happening and do nothing else was madness. Her priorities were her people and her planet.

With the *Enterprise*'s aid, a temporary habitat was established on Toro, the smaller of the Vesbian moons. But this was not a permanent solution. After the initial asteroid strike, those in the lunar habitat would have to be transported back to the planet surface where they must take their chances. Yes, relief ships would come from Starbase Twelve, but there were not enough resources in the entire sector to keep the colony supplied indefinitely. Mister Spock had estimated that the Federation could supply aid for approximately a year after the disaster, but at that point there was nothing more that could be done without the expenditure of enormous resources. Vesbius was simply too far away from the heart of the Federation for mass transport of goods. The colonists would either have to come up with a solution, or they would slowly die of starvation and lack of medical supplies.

The problem was, there simply were not enough ships. Hannah had counted and recounted the berth spaces, calculated what it would take to cram every nook and cranny with people, to no avail. The numbers did not match up.

There were five thousand to be evacuated, and there were twenty-eight hundred spaces available. She knew the *Enterprise* could temporarily take two thousand. Kirk had said that was his absolute upper limit, which was barely sustainable for a day or so. Multiple trips to the Toro habitat would deliver three hundred more. The remaining ships, shuttle-craft included, accounted for, at most, five hundred more slots.

That left twenty-two hundred souls with no means of escape.

One thing Hannah was sure of was that none of those who must remain would be children. But, because Vesbian had such a fertile population, a good portion of those without berths must, nonetheless, be mothers or fathers of Vesbian children.

Those children were going to lose a parent, perhaps both. There simply were not enough single and childless people to substitute, even though almost all of those who were had volunteered to remain on the surface.

She herself would be among those remaining on the surface.

The settlers who were evacuating or sending off children had moved away from their homes and were beginning to assemble in tent-covered enclaves near the ships. Among these were many families, for although some parents had decided to leave the children in the shelters and take the ships away, others had decided the family must remain united. The choice was up to them. Hannah had made the plea to the Planetary Council that parents should be the ones who made the decision, and the Council had acquiesced. But the failure of the auto-immune rejection drugs had made clear that if the children left Vesbius for a lengthy amount of time, they would be the first to experience the rejection response that had almost killed Hannah on the trip to Janus VI.

As Hannah passed among the refugee tents of the waiting families, many eyes followed her, particularly the eyes of children. She stopped here and there to pat a head or say hello. One little girl was playing with a doll, and Hannah joined her for a while, losing herself in the familiar childhood ritual. But then the little girl asked her, "What is it like in space?" She pointed to her doll. "Is Jillie going to like it?"

It took Hannah a moment to swallow the lump in her throat and reply.

"Jillie might be a little frightened," she said, "but she will not have to be there long. And then you and she will be back on the ground and we will take care of you."

Somehow or another, Hannah thought, *I swear that we will.*

Two days until impact. It had seemed, at least momentarily, that the Exos movement on the planet was stymied, if not disbanded, as the last of the days before the asteroid arrived were upon them all—at least Hannah had hoped so. But her hopes proved to be misplaced. As she got into her transport sled to make her weary way back to the capital complex, Hannah received an emergency call from Fussdesberge, a wealthy and environmentally blessed sector of the settlement near a rushing river that fell from the mountains and fed the rich barley fields below.

Ferlein, recovered and faithful as always, remained with her as a bodyguard. Her father had replaced Hox with a woman from his own security detail. Hannah had gone to school with her, though they had not gotten along back then. Frances Meredith was a by-the-book, rule-following sort, and Hannah was a free spirit. While their personal relationship might be prickly, Hannah didn't have the slightest doubt Meredith would defend her to the death.

Another lesson learned, Hannah thought. *Trust your own intuition over some applicant's impressive résumé.*

They arrived at dusk at the Fussdesberge courthouse, just as the moons were rising. A scene of pandemonium stretched out below. People from the countryside surrounded the courthouse steps. They held up lighted nightsticks, the illumination source commonly used for evening travel in the colony, and several groups gathered around roaring bonfires. Hannah could not be sure, but as they swooped in closer, they seemed to be burning straw effigies and, here and there, a Planetary Council flag.

All the makings of an angry mob, Hannah thought.

Meredith flew the sled into their midst, and the crowd parted reluctantly before the big sled shoved them aside with its antigrav pulsars. They landed at the base of the courthouse steps, and Hannah stepped off the sled and walked up to the courthouse door.

Xart, the district's chief gendarme, stood there. He was a minor party official and had received his appointment as a sinecure after his father's political group had won the previous election. Xart was a slight man and did not look the part of a policeman. In fact, he appeared to be about to throw up his dinner.

"I don't know what to do, ma'am," the man proclaimed upon seeing Hannah. "They started showing up just after the court finished its final session. Most of these are not from around here—seems like they've been sledded in."

"Are they making demands?" asked Hannah.

"Sure they are," said the gendarme. "They want Bellamy Hox released—that's what they want. They want him free."

"Hox?" said Hannah. "On what grounds?"

"The sentence came in today," said Xart. "He was found guilty of attempted murder, of *you*, ma'am. The judge wasn't sure what to do with him, since anywhere we put him would be taking up the space for an innocent person. So she decided—"

The judge stepped out of the doorway and Hannah recognized her as Ellen Freitag, an old friend of her mother's and one of the leaders of the expedition that had originally settled the planet. "I decided that the scumbag could stay on the surface in jail and take his chances. After that, we'll ship him off planet to a penal colony. He can take his chances with the autoimmune vaccine. Maybe there will be an improved version by then."

"That seems . . . harsh," said Hannah.

"A Federation colony will be able to help him much better than we can here, particularly considering our current circumstances. As a matter of fact, I've arranged for him to be taken away in the brig of the *Enterprise*." Freitag chuckled. She was known for her tough sentences and for running a fair courtroom, but she was no politician.

The last thing they needed at the moment, reflected Hannah, was a judge lecturing this group on the fact that they had no right to challenge a ruling that was effectively a death sentence for the convicted.

On the other hand, nearly two thousand innocents were under a death sentence at the moment, and *they* had not tried to kill fifteen Horta and Hannah herself.

"Give us Hox!" cried someone in the crowd.

"He was trying to save Vesbius!" shouted another.

"Yes, exactly. That is exactly right." It was a voice Hannah recognized. The front of the crowd parted, and Jasper Torn stepped forward from the mob. "Why don't you get us off this hellhole permanently? It's the least you can do after causing such a good man to suffer."

"Jasper?" gasped Hannah. "You are a Planetary Council member. You have to realize this is madness!"

"What I realize is that the time has come to bring everything out in the open, Hannah Faber," he said. His constant supercilious smile never left his handsome face. "We demand an end to sham democracy and cowering. Let the strong survive. And if you will not grant it, we will *bring you down*."

He turned to the crowd and held up a fist in the air, then opened it into five outstretched fingers.

Everyone knew what he was doing. This was the salute of the Exos movement.

"Jasper! You've joined the Exos?"

Torn turned and smiled at Hannah. "I *am* the Exos. Don't you see, Advisor? Do you really think Hox and Merling acted alone? Do you think the shelter bombs planted themselves?"

This was too much for Ferlein and Meredith.

Their hands brought phasers from hidden pockets, and these were pointed at Torn.

"No," said Hannah to her bodyguards. "Lower your weapons." She turned back to Torn. "What are you saying, Jasper? What have you done?"

"What needs to be said," Torn replied. "And now we will again do what needs to be done."

He turned to the mob. "Are you with me?" he shouted.

"Yes!" a ragged chorus called back.

Hannah had been his political opponent, but she had not suspected Jasper Torn of being a terrorist, much less the mastermind of Exos. But Hannah was not surprised by the mob sentiment. Since she had been back, the call for freeing Hox had grown.

More shouts arose from below the courthouse steps, and a rotten apple flew by, barely missing Hannah's head. Soon they would be throwing harder material. Hannah knew that she had to do something to oppose these calls for vigilante justice. If Xart wasn't going to help her—and it was very apparent that he was scared out of his boots—then she would have to do it alone.

Ferlein and Meredith moved to stand on either side of her. "We have to get you out of here, ma'am," said Ferlein, scowling over the mob.

"No," Hannah said. "That I will not do."

But what action *could* she take?

Then the problem was solved for her.

"Statement! A statement for the press!" It was Johnny Sanchez, a reporter for the *Daily Buzz*. Sanchez was a one-time Exos supporter who had supposedly "reformed" and now passed himself off as a serious journalist. Hannah knew he was clever and amusing, and he had developed quite a following. His newsfeed was the third most popular on the planet. Many of the planet's residents had the *Daily Buzz* set to receive on their portable communicators. Through him, Hannah could talk directly to the people, if she could get past Torn.

He appeared to be primping, attempting to maneuver his way between Hannah and Sanchez. The reporter had himself hardwired with recording devices.

"Yes, Johnny," Torn said. "Finally, the time has come—"

"The Council member forgets himself," Hannah said loudly, cutting off Torn's oration and moving up beside him. "I have a message from the chancellor's office, and I have a victim's statement."

Sanchez immediately turned to face her. Here was better news than some minor Council member's speechifying.

"The fact that Bellamy Hox almost killed me makes no difference in the larger scheme of things," said Hannah. "If it had not been for Doctor McCoy, I would be dead. Yet I believe I was only an afterthought for Hox and the Exos terrorist movement."

Cries of "Lies!" and "Release Hox!" But there were a few in the crowd who had begun to listen. Some even appeared to realize that Hannah was responding intelligently and coherently, and she was not merely shaking a fist at them.

"The target of Hox and his accomplice, Major Johan Merling, was another species, an intelligent, thinking, and *feeling* species. They are called the Horta. They may be utterly different from us, but they are allies, and we will soon owe these creatures our lives. And maybe someday we shall call them friends. They deserve justice, and I believe justice has been served today."

"Alien scum!" shouted Torn. He moved toward Hannah as if to finish what Hox had started, but Ferlein and Meredith quickly interposed themselves. "Give us Hox!" he contented himself with shouting. "Give us Hox!"

Hannah smiled and continued addressing Sanchez. The newsman stood one step below her and was looking up at her. He appeared mesmerized, whether by her beauty or the scoop he was getting, it was impossible to say. From his position, Hannah figured the vid was showing her at a commanding angle. Good.

"Aliens? Absolutely, the Horta are aliens," Hannah said. "But the greatest victim of Hox and Merling was not alien at all." She reached down and put a hand on Sanchez's shoulder, looked him as deeply in the eyes as she could, and addressed Sanchez and his audience. "These criminals' greatest victim was *you,* the citizens of this colony. In attempting to destroy the Horta, they were attempting to murder Vesbius herself—our beloved planet—for all time."

Lieutenant Uhura was monitoring the *Daily Buzz* feed on the *Enterprise.* She turned to the captain, saying, "There's an interesting development on the planet, sir."

"Can it wait?"

"I think you should see this, Captain," said Uhura. "Shall I pull it up on viewscreen?"

Kirk turned to his communications chief. Uhura understood the demands on his time and she didn't make such requests without good reason. He nodded his assent, and she keyed the newsfeed to the main viewscreen.

Hannah was on the steps of some government building. The feed vid revealed a crowd surrounding her.

No, not a crowd, thought Kirk. *A mob.*

What was she up to?

Kirk watched as Hannah tried to talk down the mob singlehandedly.

Then a challenger appeared, a man Kirk thought he recognized.

Hannah's response.

The crowd's disdain.

They're not going to kill her. Not on my watch, Kirk thought.

"Spock, you have the conn," said Kirk. He turned to Uhura. "Have a ten-member security team meet me in the transporter room on the double, Lieutenant. We're going down to the planet surface."

Captain's log, Stardate 6417.1. Concerned that the Exos terrorist movement is trying to seize control of Vesbius, I have beamed down to the Vesbian colony in order to prevent a mob from freeing would-be assassin Bellamy Hox. He was found to have links to an Exos terrorist organization and, while acting under some personal duress, was found guilty of sixteen counts of attempted murder for the ideological cause of genetic supremacy. The moral dilemma created by the genetic engineering of humans has resulted in political turmoil and factionalism. It seems that in the attempt to create paradise, humanity cannot help but breed toxic weeds as well.

"Listen to me," said Hannah. "I bear Bellamy Hox no ill will. It is true that he was threatened by the death of his family to do what he did, and I forgive him. But to *forget* what he has done, to let him get away with doing this, and to open ourselves to the possibility he will do so again—this we cannot permit."

Hannah looked out over the crowd. Far from being mollified, the mob seemed to surge toward her. They were coming for her. She had failed.

Nearby, Jasper Torn laughed. "Did you really think you could fight those who are your superiors?" he roared.

Hannah ignored him, but she flinched at the mob's approach.

Ferlein and Meredith placed themselves two steps down from her, ready to defend her with their lives.

There were too many out there, and many of them were just as well armed as her bodyguards. The mob would make short work of them all once it surged.

So this is the end, she thought. *I don't even get to find out if the asteroid was diverted. Or to see* him *one last time.*

Suddenly, between her and the mob a line of men and women with drawn phasers materialized. It took Hannah a moment to recognize that this was Jim and an *Enterprise* security detail.

"Stand ready," Kirk ordered as soon as he had fully materialized. The *Enterprise* crew formed a phalanx that looked forbidding. The sight of a row of phasers pointing straight at them caused the crowd to step back. But still they did not disperse.

No, no, thought Hannah. *This is not the way. This will solve nothing.*

"Jim, what are you doing? Firing will only make things worse in the long run."

Kirk turned away from the mob and looked at Hannah. "I can't let them storm up here and kill you . . ."

"Yes, please, Captain, shoot them," said Jasper Torn. "Go ahead and shoot them all. And then watch us rise up and destroy you." The man laughed. "We *are* the superior beings. You understand this, don't you, Captain? You know it in your bones."

Wasn't this the Council member Torn, who'd spoken to us before? The one who'd reminded me of Khan?

"I made the mistake of indulging an Augment for too long in his fantasies once," said Kirk. "I won't make that mistake again."

Kirk raised his phaser and fired point-blank at Torn with the phaser on stun. The man crumpled onto the courthouse steps, stunned into unconsciousness by the phaser blast.

The mob roared at the sight and surged forward. But the *Enterprise*'s security detail, now joined by Ferlein and Meredith, held their ground and stared resolve straight back at them.

"You have to give me another chance," Hannah

begged Kirk. "I have to get to them, or this will spiral out of control."

If anybody had a chance, it would be Hannah Faber. In another universe, Kirk reflected, she might've made a hell of a starship captain.

"All right, talk to them," he said. "Nobody's taking that prisoner anywhere. I have the ability to beam Hox up at any time and throw him in the brig."

"Yes, Jim, I know." Hannah touched his arm. "He's only a minor matter now, however."

Hannah walked down the three steps to the officers forming the security detail and put her hand on a leveled phaser. The security officer looked to Kirk, who nodded. The man allowed Hannah to lower his weapon. And then the next allowed her to do the same, and the next, and the next, and the next, and, finally, Hannah's own bodyguards.

This was not lost on the crowd: Hannah's actions seemed to have a far greater effect than any of her words. The crowd's incessant murmur began to moderate to a more conciliatory tone. When she had pushed all the phasers down and they were hanging harmless, Hannah mounted the stairs once more and turned to address those gathered. They had grown respectfully silent, waiting to hear her, a crowd instead of a mob.

Still, much would depend on what Hannah said next.

"Live and let live," Hannah began. "We are a

world where you can do what you want and make your way as you choose. A world where the bureaucratic rules of the galaxy do not apply. There is only one law we have ever needed here: Live and let live.

"Freedom can only exist where others do not determine our fate for us. Murderers take that away from us, and they do not deserve to go free.

"Live and let live. Bellamy Hox couldn't do it. He couldn't follow the one rule, the one code, which makes us Vesbians. That's why he can't be among us anymore."

Hannah's speech, amplified and carried over the newsfeed by the reporter, seemed to have a slow ripple effect across the gathered crowd. Many now were nodding their heads in agreement. There were one or two more shouts of abuse, but the crowd began to disperse. With the *Enterprise*'s security officers standing a mute guard, Hannah and Kirk watched from the courthouse steps as the people left.

Hannah moved closer to Kirk and whispered in his ear, "Remember our dance? The kiss on the veranda?"

"Yes."

"So simple and easy," she said. "Nothing will ever be that simple and easy again."

"No," Kirk said.

"No," whispered Hannah.

It was in this moment that Kirk knew that, aside from all biological and physiological reasons, Hannah must remain here with her people. Asteroid strike or no, this society was at a crossroads. It could go the way of peaceful coexistence with the humanity it had left behind, or it could go the way of Khan and his Augments. Hannah represented the way of peace. She had a destiny, and she must see the people of this planet through to a new dawn.

"Hannah, I'll leave the detail here overnight to guard the building. Hox will not be sprung from his cell. He will not become an Exos rallying point."

"Thank you," Hannah said.

"What do you want done with . . ." He touched his boot to Torn's prone body. It might be morning before the man regained consciousness.

"Jasper Torn. He is—was—a member of the Planetary Council."

"Shall I take him back to *Enterprise*?" the captain asked.

"No, Jim, you must let him go," Hannah said.

"Hannah, he's dangerous."

"I know," she said. "You must leave this matter to us." She smiled a conspiratorial smile. "Torn is a fool. He'll lead my people to the others. We'll gut the Exos from the inside out."

"He's a fool who nearly had you killed," Kirk said. "You're playing with fire."

"Politics is nothing else but playing with fire, Jim," Hannah replied sweetly.

"I have to get back to my ship. There's much to do."

Hannah nodded sadly. "Yes, I must get back to my people. The shelters are almost ready, and the ships must be tended. Goodbye, James T. Kirk."

"Goodbye, Hannah."

Kirk had barely settled into his captain's chair upon returning to the bridge when Spock approached him.

"Captain, may I speak with you?" Spock asked.

"Of course."

"While I was negotiating with the Horta, Slider Dan offered me an interesting proposition," Spock began. "Using the data Mister Scott has compiled from his seismic survey, I have been able to alter the dig pattern of the Horta. It's my belief that, with these new parameters, we will save twelve hours from the time required to complete the asteroid coring."

"But you have more to say? Go on."

"Yes, sir," Spock continued. "Slider Dan expressed reservations about the colonists' preparations of their underground shelters."

"How does he know about them?"

"I told him, sir."

"When?"

"After his rescue. He is a very inquisitive being, sir," Spock said. "One most given to curiosity."

"He thinks the tunnels won't work?"

"He likened them to an eggshell under a boot heel."

"Could he be mistaken?"

"Undoubtedly he could be," said Spock. "But the Horta possess a certain . . . intuition when it comes to matters of digging."

"What did he propose?"

"To enlarge the planetary tunnels and shore them up on a crystalline level. In the process, the Horta may be able to create the shelter space needed to at least allow the stranded settlers to weather the initial strike."

"The Horta can dig enough space for thirty-two hundred people in half a day?"

"Slider Dan called it child's play, sir," Spock replied.

"Some of the colonists won't like it," said Kirk.

"There is one other consideration," Spock said. "I have been unable to factor in time for evacuation of the Horta, should we beam them down."

"The Horta on the planet would have to weather the asteroid strike along with the Vesbians?"

"That is correct," Spock replied.

Not all the clans volunteered. The Tunnel Borers couldn't be bothered, but many of the Sand Blasters had decided to come along.

And then there was Star Clan. Slider Dan liked the name of his newly created, very small family. The links of the other four Horta affiliations truly were broken, and a new clan was formed. Slider Dan now felt shame for the selfishness of his Tunnel Borer kindred, although he would always take pride in the clan he'd been born to.

However, his current clan membership was far more satisfying. The Star Clan Horta seemed to have more . . . more individuality than any Horta he had ever encountered, excepting the All Mother herself.

Was this what it meant to grow up?

All might be for naught. They had taken on a daunting assignment, and an asteroid strike was nothing to trifle with. A Horta could withstand enormous stress, but Slider Dan knew that there were limits. The All Mother had taught them as much. Pure magma was death. A Horta could dissolve in minutes, possibly seconds, depending on the surrounding temperature.

A direct hit in the immediate vicinity would create a raging caldera of enormous proportions.

And yet here they were under the surface of Vesbius, attempting to help out. This made Slider Dan feel . . . very useful. He liked that feeling. Daring, even.

"They don't seem to care for us much," said Missile-in-Rock, Slider Dan's Star Clan compatriot.

She was working the wall beside him. Star Clan had given the Sand Blasters the honor of digging deeper, and they were concentrating on shoring the walls in the caverns the humans had already created.

"It's natural," Hot-John, a former Melter Clan member, replied. "They are hideous in appearance and they likely are embarrassed and shrink from our view."

Slider Dan blew a puff of steam from an anterior orifice, the Horta equivalent of a chuckle. "I do not think so," he said. "It is *we* who appear hideous to them."

"Impossible," said a former Sand Blaster male, Crumblecake. "The miners like us well enough."

"These are not the people of Janus VI," said Slider Dan.

As if to prove his point, a human child who was wandering by in the corridor approached Missile-in-Rock. She prepared for the human's touch, which she expected to enjoy, and thought she might even caress the little one in turn.

This was interrupted by a scream from behind the child. Adult creatures, presumably the small human's parents, charged after the little one. They arrived just as it was about to touch Missile-in-Rock and yanked it away so forcefully that the child made a sound of startled outrage like gas from an escaping constriction point. The larger humans dragged the smaller one away as quickly as they could, casting glances back over their oddly shaped carapaces; Slider Dan supposed it was to ensure that no Horta were following them.

"Missile-in-Rock would not have harmed you," Slider Dan called after the retreating Vesbians, but to no avail. There was no common communication, and no time to establish the methods used with the Janus VI miners.

"Primitives," said Crumblecake. "They probably think we are lavagoblins or an escaped Ghost-in-the-Rock." These were underground monsters from frightening tales that the All Mother had told the Horta to entertain them during rest shifts. Nobody older than six months believed them. Slider Dan was not so sure they might not have some basis in truth, but he didn't want to bring that up now.

"They are afraid for their young one, nothing more," he said. "Not so different from us."

"If you say so," Missile-in-Rock replied. Huffing out a derisive laugh of steam, she returned to shoring the tunnel. It was funny what the humans thought was secure. These tunnels were fairly well constructed by human standards, but by Horta standards they were claptrap affairs of almost no utility.

The deeper tunnels the Sand Blasters were digging would be *much* stronger and much wider than these narrow corridors.

But when Slider Dan of the Star Clan was

finished with the existing shelter corridors, he'd wager a mountain of geodes that his walls could withstand anything. If the asteroid could not be averted, the Horta would have a chance to test his wager.

Provided they survived. If they did not, Slider Dan thought ruefully, Speaker from the Stars was going to have some explaining to do to the All Mother.

I'll have to see that everyone makes it, Slider Dan thought. *For I would never wish to put Speaker from the Stars in such a position.*

Anyway, he was planning to ask the Speaker from the Stars for a favor. Slider Dan had made up his mind to apply to Starfleet Academy.

Sixteen

Captain's log, Stardate 6418.4. The Horta have completed coring the asteroid headed toward Vesbius. In a brave and inspired move, a number of the Horta have volunteered to shore up and dig deeper the fallout shelters on the planet's surface. They have accomplished this quickly, and the thousands of Vesbians who would have been stranded without shelter in the event of an asteroid strike are now underground. However, there is no time to evacuate the Horta volunteers—a condition the Horta understood when they beamed down.

The Enterprise *must now attempt to complete the destruction and deflection of the asteroid using our phasers and tractor beams. The success of this operation is far from certain.*

The correct moment to blast the asteroid was after it passed within the orbital radii of the planetary moons. Spock had factored in the tidal force of the moons so they could aid in asteroid breakup—this was the way he had achieved his grant of extra hours needed to deploy the Horta digger teams on Vesbius.

With the extra space the Horta had created, it had not been necessary to pack the *Enterprise* with two thousand colonists. With the option to enter the shelters, far fewer Vesbians had elected to leave the planet, and the *Enterprise* was carrying only two hundred and sixty evacuees—a population easily accommodated on a temporary basis. But "temporary" was the watchword, for within days they would all begin to experience the autoimmune response that would doom them, and so they must return to their planet.

Provided there was a livable planet to return to.

Captain Kirk wondered what he would do if there was not. He couldn't imagine he would merely watch them slowly die, but absent a medical breakthrough, what choice would he have?

The *Enterprise* bridge was alive with activity. The time had come. The Horta had completed their task. Scotty had brought his tunnel buggy back, and, at the request of the Horta, was planning to deliver it to the mining colony at Janus VI. The rover might not only prove useful on Janus VI, but it would be a reminder of the friendship the Horta had formed with the engineer.

"Spock, report," said Kirk as he settled into the command chair that Spock had just vacated.

"Horta operations planet side are now complete,

sir," said her Spock. "All settlers reported within the shelters. In 3.7 minutes we will be ready to proceed with the asteroid destruction operation."

"Very good, Spock. All the Horta are accounted for?"

Spock raised an eyebrow. "Yes," Spock said. "I have accounted for every last one of them."

Kirk smiled. "Of course you have, Spock." Kirk grew more serious. "Let's get this operation under way then."

The captain keyed his intership communications. "Mister Scott, have you got our firing solutions uploaded to the main computer?"

"Firing solutions uploaded and ready, Captain," said Scotty.

"Very well. Stand by." Kirk turned to Sulu at the helm weapons station. "Do you have phaser lock, Mister Sulu?"

"Phaser lock established, Captain," reported Sulu.

"Mister Spock, final report on the Horta?"

"All Horta secured, all Vesbians accounted for," said Spock.

The main viewscreen showed the asteroid speeding through the starry sky. It didn't look any different. Although a host of Horta had been released upon it and they had honeycombed the monstrosity in a thousand different directions, it was still one huge mass of rock. The *Enterprise* was dwarfed beside it.

For a moment, Kirk shook his head in wonder at the audacity of their plan. *Let's just hope it's enough.*

"Mister Sulu," Kirk said. "Fire phasers."

There was the familiar power surge, then the squeal of the phasers.

"Phaser bank one fired, sir," said Sulu.

Kirk looked at the asteroid on the viewscreen. Nothing. The phaser seemed to have no effect whatsoever.

"Fire phaser bank number two," said Kirk.

"Firing phaser bank number two," Sulu replied, and he pressed the button adjacent to the one he had just depressed.

This time the effect was dramatic.

The asteroid began to break apart. At first there was only a tiny crack formed at the point of contact with the phaser blast. But this crack began to spread in a hundred different directions, then in thousands. The last point of the initial phaser blast served as a destination for these cracks to travel from. Kirk realized that what he was seeing was the breaking up of the asteroid along the lines that the Horta had dug. It was cracking up, as it was expected, as it needed to.

This might just work!

"The asteroid is separating along projected lines," Spock reported. "Sensors indicate that the mass is breaking up in chunks manageable by our tractor beams."

"Excellent," said Kirk. "Chekov, tractor beams.

Sync them with the sensors and let's clear that thing away."

"Aye, sir," said Ensign Chekov.

The ensign began applying the tractor beams to the various masses. Sulu made minute course adjustments. The two worked together, reading each other's moves. It was as if they had been born to maneuver a starship.

As he watched, Kirk could see the asteroid debris field being pushed away. The lift door opened, and Scotty exited. He looked at the viewer and nodded with satisfaction.

Chekov and Sulu maneuvered a particularly large mass using the tractor beam combined with the *Enterprise*'s impulse engines. The chunk spun out on a course that was outside of the system and into deep space.

As Scott watched the readings from the engineering station, his smile turned to a look of concern. "Captain, we have a problem."

"What is it?" asked Kirk.

"The center mass. It hasn't broken up the way that we planned."

Kirk immediately saw what Scotty was talking about. It seemed relatively small, a tiny mass at the center of the exploded asteroid. Surely that couldn't be a problem.

But Kirk's every spacefaring instinct told him it *could* and that it *was*.

"That center is dense. It's composed of iron and nickel. I believe it's too big to move with our tractor beams."

"Mister Spock?" Kirk demanded of his science officer.

"Tensile strength is too great for either our phasers or photon torpedoes to have effect," Spock reported. "The specific mass would absorb a photon torpedo barrage. We would damage the surface, perhaps even split it into pieces, but it would not be sufficient to change its trajectory enough to avoid planet fall."

"Where's it going to hit?"

"It is headed for the main population center," Spock said. "It will hit in two minutes."

"Notify the colony," Kirk said to Uhura.

"Aye, sir."

"Damage estimate," Kirk ordered.

"Captain, the diameter of that asteroid piece is one hundred and twenty-one meters."

We got so much of it, said Kirk to himself.

"Captain, there will be atmospheric contact in forty-five seconds," said Spock.

"Follow it in. Blast it out of the sky," said Kirk.

Sulu and Chekov moved to execute his orders, and the *Enterprise* drew closer, phasers blasting away.

It was no use. The surface was scored, but it was not broken apart. Its velocity was too great to be halted by applied tractor beams.

"Hull temperature increasing," said Scotty from the engineering station. "Captain, the *Enterprise* will burn up coming in at this angle."

"Correct course," said Kirk. "Follow that thing in as close as we can!"

They were within ten kilometers of the rock; the atmosphere was beginning to tug at the *Enterprise*.

"Captain, outside hull temperatures at maximum. Shields are down forty percent."

"One more shot, Sulu," said Kirk.

Sulu fired the phasers.

One, two, three, Kirk counted grimly.

Nothing. No effect.

"Take us about and get us out of here," Kirk ordered.

"Coming about, sir," said Sulu.

"Hull temperatures still climbing, Captain," said Scotty.

The *Enterprise* was buffeted as it hit the outer atmosphere and skipped across it like a flat stone on a lake. The only difference was that every hit of the stone on *this* lake caused an increased friction.

Hold together, Kirk thought. *Hold together, girl.*

A final wrenching buffet threw everyone into the backs of their seats as the *Enterprise* cleared the atmosphere. She was free. Safe in space.

"Establish orbit, give me a visual on that strike," said Kirk.

Sulu, who by any measure should have been

rattled, responded with his customary fluidity and brought the ship into orbit. There was a moment of blurriness as the sensors sought the correct resolution and focus, and then the planet appeared.

The first effects of the asteroid strike began. An enormous plume of dark material rose up from below into the atmosphere. First it turned a milky brown, and then, occluding a large portion of it entirely, a black cloud rose, and within that cloud rose a red flame. The flame grew into what appeared to be an angry eye in the center of darkness.

"What is that?" Kirk asked.

"A volcanic eruption of enormous magnitude," said Spock. "It appears that the asteroid fragment has dug its way to the planet's mantle and has temporarily opened the passage for the outflow of magma onto the surface. What you're witnessing is a volcanic plume approximately a hundred thousand feet high."

"Can anything survive there?" Uhura asked.

"We will discover that shortly, Lieutenant," said Spock. "The planetary puncture is closing over and the escape of magma has sealed it. There has been a rapid heating of the atmosphere by three degrees Celsius. This will linger for approximately six months, and then the cooling effect caused by the occlusion cloud will begin to take effect as sunlight is blocked. At that point there will be rapid cooling, snowstorms, and the initial formation of the glaciers that will eventually cover a good portion of the northern and southern hemispheres of this planet."

"Hannah," whispered Kirk.

"Sensors indicate that damage is far less than a full-on strike would have produced. The planetary biosphere will likely survive in some measure. Whether that will be enough to preserve the Vesbian colonists remains to be seen."

"If only there were something we could do," Uhura said.

But there was not.

Beneath the *Enterprise,* Vesbius writhed in agony.

Seventeen

Captain's log, Stardate 4915.2. The Enterprise *was able to prevent the utter destruction that a full-on asteroid strike would have brought. However, a sufficient portion of the asteroid fell on the planet. It will be years, perhaps centuries, before Vesbius fully recovers. According to our sensors, a substantial portion of the biosphere remains. The fate of the colonists and Horta digging volunteers on the planet at this time: unknown.*

The *Enterprise* landing party beamed down onto what had once been the veranda overlooking the verdant valley of the Vesbius colony. Kirk looked out upon a scene of devastation. The crops had been flattened by a pressure wave and then burned to a crisp by the eruption of the planetary magma. All smelled of sulfur and ash.

There were a few items that had escaped the cataclysm below. While the river was gone, a ragged scar now filled with dry ash, two houses out of the hundreds still stood by its ashen banks. They seemed more skeletal framework than houses.

"Spock, is there anything alive?"

Spock turned his tricorder in several directions. "Minimal macrobiology remains in this valley. Confirming the *Enterprise* sensor readings that this is the status of this world. It seems a few insect analogs have survived, particularly a ground-hugging insect similar to Earth's cockroach. There may be a sufficient gene pool to enable a recovery, in fifty or a hundred years."

"The cockroaches survived," said Kirk with chagrin.

"Captain, I do have life signs, headed in our direction at extreme velocity. Four humans and one Horta."

The landing party waited. Walking around on this devastated landscape might be dangerous. It sure was depressing.

Five minutes later the antigravity sleds arrived. In them were Chancellor Faber and his staff. Hannah was among them. She looked as changed as the planet. They landed the sleds on the ruins of the veranda and stepped off.

"Chancellor," Kirk said.

"Captain Kirk," Chancellor Faber replied. "We are very glad to see you. We're very happy to see anyone. The cooling has set in, and now the tidal wave of destruction has passed. We are crawling out of our holes. We are alive—thanks to this Horta and his compatriots."

The chancellor indicated the Horta, whom Kirk recognized as Slider Dan. The Horta shuffled in place in acknowledgment.

"We also had two shelters with cave-ins near the entrance," Faber continued. "My people would have been trapped, but for the Horta. They dug us out."

"Chancellor, it would appear that the planet's biosphere was damaged but not destroyed," said Spock. "The ecological interactions that lead to your integration with the planet's biome seem to remain intact. There may be just enough diversity remaining to support it."

"We have felt this," said the Chancellor. "And we will make it our mission to increase the diversity and bring our planet back."

Hannah stepped up next to her father.

"We also know something that your sensors cannot tell you, Mister Spock," she said. "Vesbius is hurting. She is in pain, and we feel her anguish." She looked to Kirk and smiled sadly. "Since none of you are Vesbians, you cannot experience this. We *are* a different species. We have made ourselves into something that is not human. While we did so to survive, we have given up something that can be precious and useful. We have given up our separateness. We are bound to this world now, for better or worse." She stepped next to Kirk and took his hand. "Two roads met in the woods, Captain. And we Vesbians have taken the less traveled path. Perhaps it is a good direction, perhaps not. But it is another direction from yours."

They toured the planet on the antigravity sleds and took in a vista of vast destruction. Yet even now, in the aftermath, people were emerging. Preparations were being made for the long winter to come. It would be generations before this planet knew the warmth of a true spring again. Yet the ground could still be sown with winter wheat and barley, at least for temporary sustenance.

"In five hundred years, this valley will be under a sheet of ice that will continue growing for perhaps another ten thousand," said Hannah. "All the things that we made here have been swept away, ground away. We must move south to the equatorial regions and hope the ice does not reach us there."

"You will tell your children how it once was, and they'll tell their children," Kirk replied. "That will be enough to keep hope alive."

Hannah smiled slightly. "I suppose we can take comfort that we will have a future."

They landed near what had once been a grand château. One tall stone corner remained; a shelter had been thrown up by settlers who had come to reclaim their land. Children ran about outside the hastily built structure. Kirk marveled that they were playing. Playing as if nothing had happened.

A little girl recognized Hannah and ran over to her.

"You! You're the one who said it would be all right," she called to Hannah.

Hannah took the girl's hand and tears welled in her eyes. Kirk put a hand on her shoulder. The girl stared up into her face and smiled. "You said it would be all right, and it is. I still have Mommy and Daddy. I even have my little brother," she said, shaking her head. "Well, I guess everything can't be completely all right."

"You don't mean that," Hannah said.

"I don't care what Uncle Rudolf and his friends say, I like the Horta!" said the little girl. "I wish I could have one for a pet, but Mommy says they are people and not meant for keeping." The girl noticed the antigrav sled. "Can I ride on your sled?"

Finally Hannah did smile. "I think that can be arranged," she said. "Right now, in fact. Why not? Let's go. Let's do it!"

Hannah took the little girl by her hand and, laughing and skipping together, the two went to the sled and climbed aboard. Hannah took the controls and activated them. The sled rose about a meter above the surface. "All right, hang on tight!" she called back to the little girl, and then they were away.

Kirk watched them fly over the planet's devastated surface. He watched Hannah draw away. When she was just a speck on the horizon, he flipped open his communicator.

"Kirk to *Enterprise*," he said.

"Scott here, Captain."

"Two to beam aboard, Mister Scott."

Captain's log, Stardate 4917.2. We are in orbit around the mining colony Janus VI. The Horta that we took to honeycomb the asteroid, which was on a collision course with the Vesbius colony, have now been returned to their homeworld. They have returned as heroes. The Horta were able to expand and strengthen the planetary shelters in record time. They are the saviors of the population of Vesbius.

Mister Spock, Doctor McCoy, and I are transporting down now to speak with the Horta about our agreement. Will Spock remain on Janus VI? Unresolved.

The grand chamber of the All Mother was filled with every Horta who could cram into the vast structure. Kirk, Spock, and McCoy stood on the stone dais near the middle of the cavern near the great central stalactite. They had been conducted there by a Horta honor guard, which, Spock assured the captain, was in no way intended to be threatening. Kirk found being surrounded by six Horta moving in unison on all sides a bit disconcerting, nonetheless. These Horta seemed to be very well-behaved Horta, and their synchronized movements spoke of a great deal of practice and drill.

Kirk had an auxiliary plan in place. All he had to do was press a button on his communicator and they would be beamed out. But at this depth, there was no way to achieve transporter lock. They would have to trust in the goodness of the Horta heart.

"The All Mother gives you her greetings and kind regards, Captain," said Spock. "She asked that I allow myself to mind meld with this congregation of Horta in order to report to you on its deliberations. May I have your permission?"

"Is it dangerous?" asked Kirk.

"I do not believe so," Spock replied. "Over the past few weeks, I have developed methods for integration with their hive mind, and protection of my Vulcan individuality. It is a curious phenomenon; the Horta have gotten used to me as well. There is a difference between venerating a legendary presence from the past and actually living with that person."

"Are you saying the Horta are getting tired of you, Mister Spock?"

"I have received no such indication, Captain." Spock tilted his head. "On the contrary, they seem to have grown rather fond of me. But more in the manner of doting on a favorite relative than the motherly affection they showed before."

"Very well," said Kirk. "Proceed, Mister Spock."

Kirk watched Spock stretch forth his hands, palms out, as if trying to grasp an imaginary pool of energy in the air about him. And then something strange happened. Spock's eyes rolled up in his head, and he let out a breath, as if he'd suddenly been shaken unexpectedly. But then soon after that his breathing regularized again. "Spock, are you all right?"

"Yes, Captain, Spock is all right." It was Spock's voice, but Kirk knew that this was not Spock speaking. There was softness to his words, a difference in delivery. Kirk knew the All Mother was now speaking through Spock.

Spock's eyes rolled back down, and for all intents and purposes, he looked just like Spock. That is, until he smiled, a contented and happy smile.

"Speaker from the Stars is welcome among us," said Spock's voice, confirming Kirk's suspicions. "As are you, Kirk. Kirk, the Finder, the Captain of the Night Sky." Spock's body turned to McCoy. "And you are McCoy, the Healer."

McCoy, clearly pleased with the sobriquet, nodded gallantly. "Good to see you again."

"We are reminded of you, McCoy, every spring when the magma rises and increased temperatures cause us to experience twinges within our old wound. You saved our life, but this spot still gives us trouble from time to time."

"I'm sorry to hear that," said McCoy.

"No one could've done better, Doctor McCoy," said the voice from Spock. "And for that we will always be grateful."

"You're very welcome," said McCoy.

Spock turned to Kirk. "And now I come to the matter of Speaker from the Stars. You made a promise to us, Captain Kirk. Spock agreed to this promise, and the children saw that he was sincere. All of the children saw that when they looked into his mind. But we also observed something else. We experienced Speaker from the Stars as he truly is within. He is human, also Vulcan, and a man of integrity and daring. I instructed the children to study this being, this Vulcan, as they traveled with him and to try to understand him. In the same way, Spock has attempted to understand us. And after this time among you, the children have reported back to me."

"And what have they discovered?" said Kirk. "We had misfortune befall us on the voyage. You've seen that there are evil ones among us, humans who would do wrong to others for no reason. The Vulcans are different from us, in many respects. Theirs is a planet of logic, nonviolence, and peace."

"Yes, Captain. We are aware of this. We are not so backwards as you suppose. Within this planet lie repositories of our memories written into crystals, into the structure of the rock itself. We are a literate species, a tool-using species, and, as you have discovered, an intelligent species who appreciate the strengths and differences of others."

"That has become completely apparent," said

Kirk. "And you, your children, have been invaluable in our recent efforts."

"So—the bargain."

"Yes, the bargain," said Kirk.

"We are not going to let you out of it, Captain," said the voice from Spock.

Kirk turned toward the All Mother and addressed her, although he made sure Spock could see him and mentally translate.

"I understand," Kirk answered. "I would regret losing the services of my first officer, and my friend."

"This is apparent," said the All Mother voice from Spock. "For this reason and others, I would like to propose an alteration to the terms."

"I'm listening," Kirk said.

"It seems that my children have had a grand time on this adventure. They want more. They want to become a starfaring species. I had hoped they would learn independence, but never in all my days did I expect *this* to happen. And it seems those who were expelled from your shuttle bay are the most adamant about this request. I understand that Slider Dan has even communicated with Spock about applying to the Starfleet Academy."

"Many species have attended Starfleet Academy," Kirk said.

"I for one do not understand the young anymore," said the voice from Spock. "It is a good thing that my time will be done soon. Captain Kirk, if you will agree to back our request for membership in the Federation, and if you, personally, will see to it that all my children who wish it get due consideration for entry into this Starfleet Academy, I will release your first officer from his promise to remain among us."

He was a starship captain, not a politician. In fact, Kirk had determined that if he were ever offered a promotion to rear admiral that took him away from his ship, he would turn it down.

What the All Mother was truly asking of him was for him to alter his plans for his own future. Did she realize that?

Kirk had the sneaking suspicion that not only did she realize it, she may have believed she was acting for *his* own good. Pushing yet another youngster to be all that he could be—even if the youngster in this case was already a Starfleet captain.

The last thing he ever wanted was to become some crusty admiral with a desk job on some starbase or on Earth. This was not the future Jim Kirk had envisioned for himself.

But if he were to fulfill the Horta's request, this vision of the old admiral might have to become his future. Because the requests that the Horta were making of him could only be accomplished with a measure of power and say-so within Starfleet command. In fact, one might have to become a veritable Starfleet politician to do the things the Horta desired.

"Kirk, you have remained silent for some time," said the voice from Spock. "Do you hesitate? Do we ask too much as a species? Are we not ready?"

"No," said Kirk. "This has nothing to do with you. Of course, you're ready. You've shown that you are prime candidates for admission into the Federation. As for the Academy—"

Decide, Kirk thought. *You've made a thousand life-and-death decisions before. Now you're presented with a devil's bargain by a very intelligent alien negotiator. You may have to rethink your career plans, but you get to keep Spock. Make this one. Follow your instinct, your intuition.*

"As for the Academy," continued Kirk, "I will do my absolute best to make sure that your children get their chance. Yes, this is an agreement I can and will enter into."

And with this Spock laughed—or, rather, the All Mother laughed through him. "Very well. I see that it is time to release Spock. His defenses against our group mind are perhaps not as strong as he believed them to be. Vulcan telepathy is an interesting phenomenon that we will have to study. We believe that we may have a few suggestions that we can make to help them improve this capacity and bring it to a level closer to our own."

"I'll be damned," said McCoy. "A species has something to teach the Vulcans. Never thought I'd live to see the day. And I'll bet the Vulcans didn't either."

Spock took a quick stumbling step forward and caught himself. He shook himself. "I am back," he said. "Doctor, Vulcans are entirely receptive to receiving wisdom that another species has to impart."

Kirk smiled. "You hear that, Bones? That is the sound of Vulcan humility. You could emulate it."

"When pigs fly," muttered McCoy, but he too was smiling.

Kirk shook his head. "Well, we should see who is coming back to Starbase Twelve with us."

Before Spock could ask, one of the Horta moved forward. Slider Dan. He was joined by four others.

"Star Clan wishes to take you up on your invitation, Captain," said Spock.

"Just like that?" asked Kirk.

"I believe they are quite sure," replied Spock.

The same honor guard escorted them out, and with them were the five volunteers. After many tunnels and some stooping, they arrived at the mining headquarters. After exchanging pleasantries with the station director once more, Kirk flipped open his communicator. "Kirk to *Enterprise*," he said. "Eight to beam aboard, Mister Scott."

"Eight, sir?"

"Yes. Lock on to my coordinates, and—" He looked over the five Horta who would accompany them and smiled ruefully. "I'll explain when I see you, Mister Scott. Beam us up."

The lift door on the bridge slid open, and McCoy stepped out. He approached Kirk with a data slate in his hand, and Kirk took it.

"Got in a full report via subspace on the rebuilding efforts on Vesbius," McCoy said. "The biosphere is being restored at a more rapid rate than they had imagined possible. It seems that all of that biological knowledge they've accumulated over the years was very useful. Times are going to be very tough, but they'll be all right in the long run. It's going to be a changed planet."

"Maybe those who didn't appreciate it before will appreciate it more now," said Kirk.

"That, if nothing else, marks the Vesbians as very human," McCoy answered.

Spock spun around from his station. He crossed his arms and silently nodded in agreement with McCoy's assessment. This seemed to rankle the doctor. "Spock," McCoy said, "you seemed a bit wistful since we dropped the Horta off at Starbase Twelve. Pining over your lost children?"

The captain decided that a little teasing might be in order to lift the Vulcan's mood. "Don't worry, Spock," said Kirk, "you would've made a terrible mother."

"Hear, hear," said McCoy.

Spock raised an eyebrow. "Gentlemen, undoubtedly you are correct. I might have served as an acceptable *father* figure, however. I believe I might have . . . grown into the role of patriarch. For all their excess of feeling," he continued, "the Horta do know how to keep their emotions contained—unlike some I could name. And, as I've noted before, they possess remarkably ordered and logical minds."

"Contained emotions? Ordered and logical minds? You're starting to sound like a proud papa," said Kirk.

"Hardly, Captain," Spock replied, turning back to his station.

Kirk nodded and exchanged a glance with McCoy.

"Ahead, warp factor two, Mister Sulu."

ACKNOWLEDGMENTS

Matthew Bynum, Abigail Manuel, and Meredith Frazier provided invaluable assistance. Margaret Clark, a fountain of *Trek* lore, was the perfect editor. And my wife, Rika Daniel, and my kids, Cokie and Hans, kept up my enthusiasm at all times. "Dad's writing about Horta!"

ABOUT THE AUTHOR

Tony Daniel is a science fiction writer and author of *Guardian of Night, Metaplanetary, Superluminal,* and short stories such as "A Dry, Quiet War." He is also an editor at Baen Books. He's had multiple stories in "Year's Best" anthologies, one of which, "Life on the Moon," won the Asimov's Reader's Poll Award for year's best story and was nominated for a Hugo Award.